THE GIRL WHO NEVER CAME BACK

ACBT Books
LONDON

Copyright © 2014 Amy Cross

This book is a work of fiction. Names, characters, places and incidents are either the product of the author's imagination or are used fictitiously, and any resemblance to actual persons, living or dead, events or locales is entirely coincidental.

All rights reserved. No part of this book may be used or reproduced in any manner whatsoever without prior written permission.

First published: October 2013
This edition: June 2014

Published by ACBT Books

ALSO BY AMY CROSS

Horror

Asylum
Ward Z
The Night Girl
Devil's Briar
The Devil's Photographer
Darper Danver series 1
The Vampire's Grave

Thriller

Ophelia
The Girl Who Never Came Back
The Dead and the Dying
The House of Broken Backs
Other People's Bodies

Dystopia / Science-Fiction

The Shades
Finality series 1
Mass Extinction Event series 1, 2 & 3

Fantasy / Paranormal

Dark Season series 1, 2 & 3
The Hollow Church (Abby Hart #1)
Vampire Asylum (Abby Hart #2)
Lupine Howl series 1, 2, 3 & 4
The Ghosts of London
The Werewolf's Curse
Grave Girl
Ghosts
The Library
Journey to the Library

Erotica

The Wife series 1
Broken Blue
Broken White

Contents

Part One: Floating
page 1

Part Two: Sinking
page 71

Part Three: Drowning
page 149

Part Four: Rising
page 205

THE GIRL WHO NEVER CAME BACK

AMY CROSS

"Late for what?"

"I'm going to be *late*!" she half-giggled and half-shouted, still trying to get free.

"Don't go where I can't see you," her mother said sternly.

"I won't," Charlotte said, using her one free hand to try prizing her mother's fingers from her wrist one by one.

"And don't get your dress dirty."

"I won't." She was trying to resist the urge to use her teeth to get free from her mother's grip.

"And don't..." Her mother paused, and finally she let go. "Charlotte, don't -"

"I know!" Charlotte said, turning and running out the door, almost tripping on the step in the process but just about managing to stay upright as she raced from the porch, down onto the grass and across the lawn. She was vaguely aware of her mother shouting another dumb rule after her, but she didn't have time to stop and listen. All she cared about was getting across the lawn as fast as possible. It was a hot day, and hot days meant only one thing: Charlotte was going to go and visit the witch.

"Charlotte!" Ruth called out, sitting cross-legged on the grass. "What are you doing?"

Ignoring her older sister, Charlotte ran straight past her, skillfully leaping over the dolls that Ruth had laid out on the lawn.

"Charlotte!" Ruth shouted. "Come back!"

With a grin on her face, Charlotte kept running, past her father's derelict old greenhouse and then finally through the broken wooden gate that had once marked the boundary between the garden and the tow-path that ran along the bottom of the family's land. Here, the well-manicured lawn gave way to overgrown bushes and low-hanging trees, and the sunlight that fell freely upon the lawn now had to fight its way through dense, overhanging foliage. Charlotte kept running, though, confident that she knew every raised tree-root and every errant rock that could possibly halt her progress; she was filled with the spirit and confidence of Ettolrahc, and finally she came to a halt at the very edge of the river. In fact, she almost went *too* far, and for a precarious second she tried desperately to hold her balance and keep from toppling into the water. Waving her arms out at her side as if she was trying to take off, she eventually brought herself under control and stood panting for breath as the river flowed lazily past.

"Now what?" she whispered with a grin.

Silence for a moment. Apart from the sound of the river.

And then:

"Charlotte!" Ruth called, a long way back but getting closer every second. "Wait!"

Charlotte ignored her sister, just like she ignored her every day. She knew that Ruth didn't understand the lure of the water, and that she'd arrive filled with dumb questions, snide comments and reminders of what not to do. Charlotte preferred going down to the river on days when her sister wasn't around, but she figured she could put up with her presence for a while. It wasn't that she *hated* Ruth; it was just that she found her sister to be a terrible irritation. Ruth was two years older than Charlotte, and the younger child often wondered whether those two years accounted for the gulf between their personalities. While Charlotte was carefree and adventurous, Ruth was more serious and waspish. Ruth would never understand about Ettolrahc.

Sometimes, it was almost as if there was only one of Ruth.

Charlotte, though, had her two sides. The impish, adventurous Ettolrahc urged her on to explore the world, while the cautious Charlotte worried that perhaps they should be a little careful. Both Charlottes lived in the same body, which meant that other people often made the mistake of thinking that she was just one girl. Charlotte knew, however, that there were two of her, and that this must be the factor that kept pushing her forward like some kind of unstoppable force. Sometimes, when Charlotte and Ettolrahc were in harmony, they seemed to fuse and become one happy, unstoppable girl, and those were the moments worth living for. Right now, they were merely close. Charlotte figured that either her sister never had this kind of two-sided personality, or maybe her two sides got stuck together one day and needed to be unpeeled. Whatever, Charlotte pitied Ruth a great deal.

"What are you doing?" Ruth asked breathlessly as she came to a halt several feet back from the edge of the river.

"I'm in the middle of something," Charlotte replied, aware that her inscrutability would drive Ruth up the wall.

"In the middle of what?"

Charlotte didn't answer. She was watching the light as it danced on the river's rippled surface. It seemed to be delivering a message, although she couldn't quiet fathom the meaning.

"In the middle of *what*?" Ruth demanded to know.

"Floating," Charlotte replied.

There was a pause. "Huh?"

"I'm floating through the air," Charlotte said. "You might think I'm standing still, but I'm not. I'm moving atom by atom. You just can't see it."

Ruth sighed. "Charlotte -"

"I'm floating like the light floats on the water," Charlotte continued.

"The light *doesn't* float on the water," Ruth replied dourly. "It's *reflected* off the surface. The whole reason you can see it is that it comes back at -"

"Ssshhh!" Charlotte said suddenly.

"Don't Ssshhh me!" Ruth replied indignantly.

"You'll scare it away," Charlotte continued.

"Scare *what* away?" Ruth asked. "The light? Is that what you mean?" She sighed again. "Charlotte, you're just being stupid. That's not what's happening. Not really. It just looks that way, but if you actually read about these things, you'll find that the light is just -"

"I *have* read about it," Charlotte replied, interrupting her. "Can't you see me moving? Each atom taking its turn in a very polite and ordered progress -"

"Mummy said not to play by the river," Ruth pointed out suddenly, as if their mother's decree resolved the whole debate. "She said there are two places we're not allowed to play. We're not allowed to play by the river, and we're not allowed to play next to Daddy's old shed."

"And what does Daddy say?" Charlotte asked pointedly.

"Daddy doesn't say anything," Ruth replied. "Daddy's dead."

"So we only have 50% of a decision," Charlotte replied with a smile. "Do you know what else I'm doing right now? I'm using the power of my mind to keep myself from falling faster."

"No," Ruth replied, "you're *not*! You're not falling at all. You're just standing there. Come on, get away from the edge. Mummy's in charge now, and we have to do what she says. Until we're older, anyway."

"I'm already older," Charlotte said. "I'm older than I was when you said those words, and now I'm older than I was when I started that sentence."

"Why are you always so stupid?" Ruth asked.

Charlotte didn't reply. She was watching the water, and wondering how cold it might be, and trying to ignore the very faint pain in her belly.

"Are you listening to me?" Ruth continued, clearly getting annoyed. "Mummy says -"

"Don't distract me," Charlotte said hurriedly. "I might lose concentration and fall, and it'll all be your fault. If you say another word -"

"Mummy wants -"

Opening her mouth to form a wide grin, Charlotte let herself fall forward. She heard the sound of Ruth calling after her, but it was too late, and she quickly plunged face first into the cold water, her ears filling with the whooshing sound of her body crashing through the current. She felt free, and for a moment she stayed perfectly still before finally she used her arms to turn so that she could look back up. Through the dirty water, she could just about make out the light still dancing on the river's surface, and the dappled, constantly shimmering silhouette of her sister standing sternly by the water's edge. Finally, for the first time that day, it felt as if Charlotte and Ettolrahc had come together as one mind, and everything was perfect.

Today

The sun's rays passed effortlessly through the bathroom window and dappled lazily on the surface of the bath. From beneath that surface, the light looked broken. Far below, with her bare back pressed against the rough bathmat as she counted out the seconds with well-rehearsed precision, Charlotte stared up and wondered if today might finally be the day that the spell would be broken. All she wanted was to find her lost half again, the half that had disappeared almost two decades earlier.

She waited.
And she waited.
Holding her breath.

She still remembered the day two decades ago when her other half had died. It had been a Saturday morning, just before the change and just before her disappearance. She remembered it so clearly; well, she *sort* of remembered, anyway. She'd been told the story so many times, she could barely work out which parts were genuine memories and which were conjured up by the words of others. The whole thing seemed childishly silly, and yet somewhere in the heart of the memory there seemed to be a kernel of truth. She certainly felt as if something had changed all those years ago, or as if something had left her, and now that she was in her late twenties she found herself thinking more and more about those days. The memories themselves seemed vague, as if they were playing on a movie screen and had happened to someone else, but they were all she had to think about in her solitary moments. She replayed them over and over again, looking for something she might have missed, but every time she came to the same conclusion: she *had* lost something, or someone, that day.

And she had never felt brave or adventurous since.

So now she waited underwater, even though it felt as if her lungs were about to burst. She had no choice. Naked and submerged, she tried to imagine time itself flowing through the water, curling around her naked body. She felt that if she could finally see time, she might have a better chance of wrangling it and forcing it to flow in reverse; she knew the task was almost impossible, but she couldn't stop trying. She felt so alone beneath the surface, as if she'd finally found a longed-for hideaway far from the eyes of the world. Suspended in the water, with her eyes wide open, she pretend to be dead: she dared not blink, or move a muscle. All she wanted was to appear still and unmoving, so that perhaps the fingers of time would not brush against her as they moved past. Somehow, it seemed to her that she had more chance of stopping time if she was underwater.

And yet deep down, the aching sensation of breathlessness was becoming increasingly painful and seemed more hopeless by the second. Her lungs were screaming for air, and she knew she couldn't deny them for much longer. This, she figured, must be how it felt to drown. She always secretly hoped that her body would somehow adapt, that she might be able to survive underwater forever, but she never had much luck in that regard. Wherever she had been while she was away as a child, she clearly hadn't been living underwater after all. She waited a few more seconds, holding her breath for as long as possible, ignoring the pain as it slowly turned in her chest and got bigger and bigger until finally she knew she could wait no longer without dying, and then she waited a moment longer, and a moment longer still, and then -

Staring up at the surface, she realized she could see a figure looking down at her. A child, watching from the dry world, a ghost... Not even a ghost, but the ghost of the half of Charlotte that had long since disappeared. The rotting corpse of her bravery.

"Fuck!" Charlotte gasped as she finally, suddenly, violently, broke the surface, gulping for air as water poured down from the top of her head. "Fuck! Bullshit! Fuck!"

Alone.

There was no-one else in the room.

She stared straight ahead, filled with the first flush of failure as she realized she was still in the same mundane old world from which she'd been trying to escape. Still catching her breath, she realized that the bath water, which had felt so warm an hour ago, now seemed unpleasantly cool on her skin. She considered turning the hot tap back on, but she didn't want to commit to a longer soak. The moment was over, so she figured she might as well get out. She just needed to summon the energy to lift herself out of the bath. Sometimes, however, that energy proved elusive; many days, she just soaked and soaked in the cooling water, wasting hours as she stared at the wall. She knew this wasn't exactly normal behavior, but she no longer cared. Besides, when she was out in public, she always put on a more energetic persona.

Leaning over the side of the bath, she looked down at the bare wooden floor and saw that it was bone dry. A slow, sly smile crossed her lips. This, at least, was a small comfort.

The fact was, the bath had been filled to the brim, with the water just millimeters from the top, before Charlotte had climbed in. A normal person would have displaced some of the water upon submerging herself, spilling onto the floor. After soaking for a while, she'd dipped her entire form beneath the surface and held it there for several minutes, enjoying the feeling of the water slowly become more and more still around her. She was up now, of course, but as she stared down at the wooden floor, she couldn't help but notice that none of the bath water had been spilled. She was used to this phenomenon, of course; it had been the same ever since the day all those years ago, when she'd first disappeared and then only half of her had come back. The water just seemed to pass straight through her body, as if it didn't notice her presence at all.

As if, despite everything, she still didn't exist.

Twenty years ago

"Why are you always trying to be weird?" Ruth asked.

Charlotte ignored the question, focusing instead on the job of patting her clothes dry. The mid-morning sun was already helping to dry her off, but she knew she wouldn't be able to fool her mother, who would undoubtedly hold a major family inquest into the incident; she also knew that she would be unable to rely upon her sister, who most certainly would be all-too-happy to squeal and tell the truth, even if Charlotte managed to come up with a decent cover story. Besides, she still had that pain in her belly, and she was feeling a little more tired than she wanted to admit. Her brief moment of union with Ettolrahc had ended as soon as she'd climbed out of the river, and they were two separate minds again.

"You're always trying to prove that you're better than me," Ruth continued, sitting on a nearby tree stump and observing her sister with a hint of cynicism in her voice. "It's like you think everyone else is stupid for being normal, and you're special because you do stupid things like jumping into a river with your clothes on."

"Go away," Charlotte muttered, shifting her attention from her clothes to her hair. Matted and unruly, she knew she could never tame it back into place, not unless she had a hairbrush. "Can you fetch something from the house for me?" she asked, turning to Ruth.

"No."

"Please? I need a hairbrush."

"Go and get it yourself."

"Mummy'll see me."

"So?"

Charlotte scowled.

"Why don't you want Mummy to see you?" Ruth asked, with a faint grin on her lips. "I thought you were the smart one, Charlotte. Didn't you have a whole plan worked out before you jumped? That's what a smart person would have done, you know. A smart person would have -"

"It doesn't matter," Charlotte replied, turning and glancing along the tow-path. "Maybe the witch'll get it for me."

"Don't say that," Ruth grumbled darkly.

"She might."

"Don't be stupid."

Charlotte smiled, realizing that she'd managed to successfully turn the tables. Her sister hated it whenever the witch was mentioned, and Charlotte knew full well that all she had to do was to keep going on about the subject for a few minutes and Ruth would turn and stomp away like an angry little baby.

"The witch probably has a hairbrush," Charlotte continued, concentrating very hard on the job of not laughing. Spotting her own shadow for a moment, she realized that the shadow was doubled over with laughter, as Ettolrahc guffawed at Ruth's stupidity. "Don't worry," Charlotte continued, "I'll just go and see her and ask if I can borrow it. Of course, she'll probably want something in return, but I suppose I can think of something. There must be a way to get her to help me, don't you think?"

"You're so stupid," Ruth replied, fixing her with a vengeful stare.

"No," Charlotte said, "*you're* stupid, because you've never seen the witch. She's down there, though. She stays well back, at the bottom of the cave, and she only lets you see her if she thinks you're worthy. She has very high standards, so most people have no idea she exists."

"And I suppose you're special enough, are you?" Ruth replied. "You're the only one who's allowed to see the witch?"

"Not the *only* one," Charlotte told her, "but one of a very small number. She likes people who understand her, and most people think she's evil. She's not, though. She's a good witch, and she does nice things for people who she thinks are on her wavelength." She paused for a moment, enjoying the look of disgust on Ruth's face. "Like me," she added eventually.

"Whatever," Ruth muttered. "I'll tell Mummy if you -"

"You tell Mummy everything anyway," Charlotte said. "I don't care. Do what you want." With that, she turned and started walking along the tow-path, away from her sister and toward the cave a few hundred meters further along the river's course. She knew she could easily spend the entire morning - maybe even the entire day and evening too - arguing with Ruth, and sometimes that kind of thing was fun, but right now she just wanted to be on her own. Sometimes, just sometimes, it seemed as if there was more to life than playing.

"Come back here!" Ruth shouted. "Charlotte!"

Instead of replying, Charlotte just kept walking, with a big grin on her face.

"Get back here right now!" Ruth screamed, her voice filled with every ounce of indignation and anger she could muster, as if she was channeling their mother's overbearing, authoritarian personality. "Charlotte, get back here! Right now! Don't go another step!"

Once she was around the bend, Charlotte stopped and looked over her shoulder. She half-expected Ruth to come running after her, but finally she realized that her sister had probably gone and run back to the house. Within a few minutes, her mother would undoubtedly be listening in stunned silence as Ruth recounted every one of Charlotte's transgressions. One side of Charlotte wanted to run after Ruth, wrestle her to the ground and prevent her from ratting her out; the other side of Charlotte, however, was determined to keep going and at least reach the edge of the cave, even if she didn't go all the way inside.

It only took a few minutes for her to reach the spot where the tow-path took a long curl to the left, with the cave partially hidden to one side. Charlotte had been to this spot many times in the past, of course, but she'd never dared to go further. This was the one point upon which her more adventurous side was never able to prevail; Charlotte's cautious side always won the argument and prevented them from going into the darkness, although they often loitered at the edge, and - like today - Charlotte enjoyed the thrill she felt every time she even contemplated going all the way into the cave and perhaps meeting the witch. Ettolrahc, of course, was screaming at her to be brave, to go all the way in and demand to see the witch face-to-face, but Charlotte felt that this was the ultimate adventure, and that as such it had to wait until she was ready.

She couldn't see the witch right now, of course, nor could she hear her. She knew she was there, though. It was as if the most powerful presence in all the world was waiting just beyond the shadows, staring out at her.

"One day," she whispered, hoping to calm Ettolrahc's desire to go rushing ahead. "I promise we'll go in one day."

Today

"Auntie Charlotte," Sophie said, shielding her eyes from the late morning sun, "why don't *you* have any children?"

Charlotte opened her mouth to reply, but at the last moment she paused, before turning to check her sister's reaction. Ruth, as per usual, looked distinctly unimpressed as she refilled her glass of lemonade and focused her attention on the magazine in her hands. Recognizing an opportunity to sow discord, Charlotte turned back to Sophie and paused for a moment, trying to work out exactly what to say.

"What makes you think I *don't* have any children?" she asked eventually.

"You don't," the girl said, wrinkling her nose for a moment. For an eight-year-old, she was remarkably direct and precocious. She was holding a chocolate biscuit in one hand, but although she brought it close to her mouth a couple of times, she never quite took a bite, as if she was too distracted by her aunt's claim. "I know you don't have any children," she added uncertainly. "You just don't."

"But how can you be sure?" Charlotte continued, deliberately teasing her niece.

There was a pause as Sophie thought about this for a moment.

"I've never seen any," the young girl said eventually, with utmost seriousness.

"Maybe that's because I keep them all locked in a dungeon," Charlotte explained, just about managing to keep from smiling. "I've actually got twenty children, Sophie, but I never let them out in the daylight. I could never take that risk."

Sophie stared back at her, her mouth open as if she was about to ask a question.

"Do you want to know *why* I can never let them out in daylight?" Sophie continued eventually.

Cautiously, hesitantly, as if she wasn't sure whether to believe her aunt or not, Sophie nodded. She was still at that age where it was possible to pull her leg and make her get reality and fantasy a little muddled together. Raising the biscuit to her mouth once more, she hesitated again, still staring at her aunt.

"It's because they're all hideously deformed," Charlotte continued, ignoring her sister's labored sigh and managing to keep from smiling. "Hunchbacks, hooked noses, peg legs, webbed feet, you name it... Every single one of my poor darlings came out a little wrong. At first, I thought they could pass in the world, so I used to dress them up in beautiful little clothes and take them into the town when I went shopping. Even though their bodies were twisted and melted and wrong, I thought they looked so beautiful with their little bonnets and their booties and shawls. I was the only one, though. Other people would run and scream, and eventually I realized that I had no choice but to hide them away from the world. There was no other way to keep them safe. I was worried the locals would turn up with pitchforks and burning torches."

"Oh, for God's sake," Ruth muttered under her breath.

"Can you believe that?" Charlotte continued. "Can you believe that people could be so mean to my poor, ugly little babies? The world is a cruel, cruel place Sophie. For people who are different, at least. For people who are ugly."

"Am I ugly?" Sophie asked tentatively.

"No," Charlotte replied with a smile. "No, you're not. Neither's your Mummy, or your Daddy, and neither am I. My poor babies, on the other hand..." She let out a theatrical sigh.

Sophie brought the chocolate biscuit to her mouth, but at the last moment she took it away again. "You don't have any children," she said quietly, clearly still doubting herself. "You're making it up."

"I'm afraid I've been a very mean and cruel mother," Charlotte added, amused by the look of rapt attention on Sophie's face, "not like your Mummy at all, and I keep all twenty of my offspring chained in my basement. It's simply the only way. I didn't want to use the chains, of course, but they were always trying to get away, and besides, if I didn't secure them, they'd scratch each other's eyes out. Several of them have already been blinded that way, unfortunately. They hate each other, you see, even more than they hate me. I keep them in the dark, so they can't see one another's horrific forms, but they call out and moan. It's quite the most horrible place in the world." She paused. "Don't worry, though. I feed them from time to time, and I torture them to keep their minds alert -"

"That's enough," Ruth said tersely, putting her glass down noisily on the table. "Jesus Christ, don't you have anything better to do?"

"She *asked*," Charlotte said, smiling as she turned and saw her sister's discomfort. "Secrets aren't healthy".

"You don't really have twenty children," Sophie said cautiously, "*do* you?"

"Have you ever been in my basement to check?" Charlotte asked.

Sophie shook her head.

"Then how do you know?" Charlotte continued. "It's all true. Ten boys and ten girls, of various ages, and I keep them chained up because..." She paused. "Well, because I like it, I suppose. Because I want to hear their moans at night. They're very good at moaning, almost like a choir. Sometimes, I think they're actually trying to harmonize -"

"Charlotte!" Ruth hissed. "Is this really necessary? You're going too far! You'll give her nightmares!"

"It's not my fault," Charlotte replied with a smile, reaching out and tousling her niece's hair. "She asked! Would you rather I lie?"

"Sophie, are you going to eat that?" Ruth asked harshly.

Sophie looked at the chocolate biscuit, which had begun to melt in her hand.

"Auntie Charlotte doesn't have *any* children," Ruth continued, pouring a glass of lemonade for her daughter before grabbing a tissue and cleaning the girl's chocolate-covered fingers. "She doesn't have a basement, and even if she did, it wouldn't be full of deformed children. She just..." Pausing, she seemed hesitant for a moment, as if she wasn't quite sure how closely to stick to the truth. "She just never had any, that's all," she said eventually. "She might do one day, but for now, she has all the time in the world to focus on her favorite person. Herself." She glanced over at Charlotte, with an expression that threatened horrific retribution if her sister didn't start to toe the line. "Isn't that *right*, Charlotte?"

"Sure," Charlotte, forcing a fake smile onto her face. "Sorry, Sophie. I'm afraid I was being kinda mean there. I don't really have twenty children locked in a basement."

"I knew you were lying," Sophie said quietly, clearly a little confused as she took a cautious bite of the biscuit.

Once Ruth had turned her attention back to the magazine she was reading, Charlotte smiled at Sophie and winked.

Sophie frowned, clearly not sure what to believe.

"Do you want to know the real reason I don't have any children?" Charlotte continued, as the sound of the nearby river drifted across the lawn.

"Why don't you go and play down by the river?" Ruth said suddenly, grabbing Sophie by the arm and forcibly turning her to face the lawn and, in the distance, the river that flowed past the house. "See if you can find any dragonflies, sweetheart. You might even find some blue ones! Wouldn't that be nice? Much nicer than sitting up here and listening to adults talk about stupid things. Anyway, I want to talk to your aunt about something." She spoke those final words with a peculiar air of menace.

"Lucky me," Charlotte muttered.

Sophie grinned.

"Go and play, sweetheart," Ruth said, waving her hand dismissively toward the river. "Go on. It'll be fun."

Sophie paused, as if she was far more interested in talking to the adults rather than obediently running down to the river. She was a slightly cautious girl, although given to occasional bursts of curiosity. In this regard, she was very much in line with the other women in her family, all of whom had in the past shown a tendency to swing between absolute conformity and occasional moments of rebellion. Sophie was still trying to find a balance between the two.

"Go on," Charlotte said with a smile. "Someone needs to keep an eye on those dragonflies, and it might as well be you. If they bite you, just bite back harder. They're mean little things, and sometimes you have to put them in their place." She glanced at Ruth, checking for the usual expression of irritation; sure enough, her sister had a face like she was chewing on a wasp. "If you see a dragonfly named Henry," Charlotte continued, turning back to Sophie, "tell him he still owes me a rabbit."

"You're silly," Sophie said with a faint smile.

"All the best people are silly," Charlotte replied.

"Go and play," Ruth said sternly.

As Sophie ran toward the river, Charlotte took a sip of lemonade before turning to her sister. She immediately realized that she was in trouble: Ruth looked even more pissed off than usual, as if she was ready to bring hell-fire down on the entire house. In a way, it was a miracle that things had been going so well. Charlotte had already spent a night in her sister's house without there being an argument, so conflict was overdue.

"I suppose you think you're smart," Ruth said eventually, with obvious disdain in her voice.

"Not particularly," Charlotte replied.

"Liar," Ruth continued, keeping her voice low as she pretended to still be reading her magazine. "You think you can just waltz in here and upset my daughter, and then waltz out again and leave me to pick up the pieces."

"If you say so."

"Not if I say so," Ruth replied. "It's the plain, unvarnished truth. You always have this smirk on your face whenever you come to my house -"

"Whenever you *invite* me, you mean," Charlotte pointed out, before a flicker of sadness arced through her chest. "What do you *want* me to tell her? That I'm a barren fuckhead? It's not like you're the goddess of fertility. You've still only plopped out one, and I know damn well that you and Tony have been trying for more."

"You're forgetting," Ruth muttered, still keeping her gaze firmly focused on the magazine, even going so far as to turn a page in order to further the impression that she was actually reading its contents, "I know you too well. If you only came to cause trouble, I don't know why you wanted to visit for the weekend at all."

"Because you and Tony begged me to come and disturb your ruinous boredom?" Charlotte replied with a smile. "God forbid that you might have to actually spend some time together." She paused, before feigning a look of shock. "My God, you might actually have to talk to your husband!"

A flicker of indignation crossed Ruth's face, but she still didn't look up from the magazine.

"What would you be doing this weekend if I hadn't come?" Charlotte asked. "You'd be plucking your own eyes out due to sheer boredom."

"Don't try to play games with me," Ruth added, finally looking over at her. "I know you too well, Charlotte. You think you can sit on the edges of my family life and take pot-shots at everything. It's true, isn't it? You think you're so fucking superior to everyone else, just because..."

Charlotte waited for her to finish. "Just because *what*?" she asked eventually, with a faint smile. She knew this was, more or less, another variation on the same argument that she and her sister had been having for more than a decade. She was faintly amused by the whole thing, although she felt a little bored. After all, Ruth wasn't exactly an inspiring sparring partner, and their bickering was well-scripted by now. In fact, Charlotte was amazed that Ruth still found the whole thing entertaining enough to keep picking these arguments.

"If you were a character in a book or a movie, no-one would like you," Ruth replied. "No-one would care about you."

"Thanks."

"And please don't upset my daughter," Ruth continued, keeping her voice low even though Sophie was now a couple of hundred meters away, playing by the riverside. "When you say silly things about having twenty children in your basement, she believes you. I know it might be hard for you to remember what it was like to be her age, but she's very credulous and it's important not to fill her mind with nonsense. I'd have hoped that as her aunt, you might be a little more willing to take her needs into account, but apparently you only care about keeping yourself thoroughly amused!" She turned another page in her magazine. "I suppose it's hard for you," she added, "adjusting to the fact that you're no longer the special one."

"The special one?" Charlotte replied, raising an eyebrow. "Why? Because I once fell off a fucking great big rock and -"

"Please don't swear," Ruth hissed, interrupting her.

"Sophie can't hear me," Charlotte pointed out, glancing across the lawn and spotting her niece playing in the grass down by the river.

"Tony and I have a new rule," Ruth continued, keeping her voice down. "We cut out all swearing, even when Sophie's not around, so that we don't accidentally slip and let her hear dirty words."

"Dirty words?" Charlotte asked, amused by the very idea. "What kind of words might those be?"

"Please don't start -"

"Shit?"

"You're twenty-eight years old," Ruth replied, clearly trying to take the moral high ground. "Please, stop being so immature."

"Could you write a list of these dirty words for me," Charlotte continued, "so I know to avoid them? I mean, some are obvious, like cunt or bollocks, but there might be some I've missed, so if you could sit down later, take out a sheet of that lovely headed notepaper you bought for yourself, and write down all these dirty words, I could memorize them and make sure never, ever to say them within a hundred miles of your precious, delicate offspring."

Silence fell between the two women for a moment.

"Sorry," Charlotte added, realizing that maybe she'd gone too far. "I didn't mean to push."

Without replying, Ruth turned another page in her magazine.

Sighing, Charlotte turned and looked back over toward the river. She expected to spot Sophie still playing in the grass, but her niece was nowhere to be seen. For a fraction of a second, a spark of concern leaped through Charlotte's chest, before she reminded herself not to be as precious and domineering as her sister. Sophie was an intelligent young girl, and Charlotte knew that she needed to be granted a little freedom. The poor girl probably had enough trouble with her over-protective parents, without needing an over-protective aunt to make things worse. Waiting for a moment to see Sophie bob back into view, Charlotte eventually decided to force herself not to be so goddamn attentive.

Leaning back in her lawn chair and trying to ignore the loud, screaming silence emanating from her sister, Charlotte finally realized that there was no way she could relax. With a faint sigh, she got to her feet, muttered something about going to check on lunch, and started to make her way toward the house. As she reached the kitchen door, she glanced back at the river, hoping to spot Sophie somewhere down there. There was no sign of the girl, however. Pausing for a moment, Charlotte reminded herself not to be as panicky as her sister. Figuring that Sophie was just out of sight, probably playing on the tow-path, she headed inside.

Twenty years ago

"You did not!" Ruth shouted, her bright blue eyes filled with pure fury. "You're a liar!"

"I did *so* go and see the witch," Charlotte snapped back, determined to wind her sister up as much as possible. She already knew that she was going to be ratted out to their mother, so she figured she'd have to get her revenge the only way she knew how: by pushing every one of Ruth's buttons until, hopefully, her sister's head would finally explode in a fit of pique. "She gave me a hairbrush and told me to tell you to stop being so mean!"

"You're not funny, you know," Ruth continued. "You're not even smart. You're just being stupid all the time, like it's some kind of hobby!"

"No," Charlotte replied, "you just -"

"You think you're being funny when you say stupid things," Ruth added, clearly warming to her theme, "but really you're just being an idiot. Everyone thinks it, Charlotte. You're the only one who thinks all these stupid things are actually impressive. Everyone else just thinks you're a stupid little idiot."

"Actually -"

"They all laugh at you behind your back," Ruth continued. "Everyone always talks about how stupid you are. They make fun of you and say that you're really stupid." She paused, getting a little out of breath. "They can all see right through you. Even Daddy!"

"Shut up about Daddy," Charlotte replied, as the pain continued to rumble in her belly. Something was wrong, but she didn't know what.

"Daddy thought you were stupid too," Ruth said with a cruel smile. "I heard Daddy talking to Mummy one day, and he was saying that he thought you were *really* dumb and that you'd probably always be dumb and you'd grow up to just be a big dumb -"

"Shut *up*!" Charlotte shouted, lunging at her sister and knocking her down onto the living room floor, before trying to pin her arms to the carpet. "Shut up!" she shouted again. "You're so -"

Before she could finish, Ruth slammed her knee into Charlotte's stomach and pushed her away, quickly following through with a kick to Charlotte's leg.

"Mummy!" Ruth shouted. "Charlotte's hitting me again!"

Charlotte turned to Ruth, ready to punch her, but at the last moment she heard the door open.

"What's going on in here?" her mother shouted. "Charlotte, what are you doing to your sister?"

"Nothing," Charlotte growled.

"She hit me," Ruth said, getting to her feet and running over to the door, while rubbing her hand over an imaginary injury on her arm. "She hit me twice because I told her she was being stupid when she jumped into the water today."

"Is that true?" her mother asked, rolling Ruth's sleeve up. "I don't see anything, darling," she said calmly, before turning to Charlotte. "Did you strike your sister?"

"No!" Charlotte shouted, close to tears but determined not to let her emotions show. "She's lying!"

"She jumped in the river," Ruth said. "Smell her hair. She stinks. And then she wanted to hide it by brushing her hair, but she didn't have a hairbrush so she went to the cave because she said the stupid imaginary witch could give her one."

Charlotte took a deep breath, trying to hold back her tears.

"Charlotte, is this true?" her mother asked.

Although she knew she should lie and claim that none of it happened, she also didn't want to give Ruth the satisfaction of thinking she'd caused her to get into trouble. She figured she might as well just own up to everything and show them both that she wasn't ashamed.

"I just wanted to go swimming," she muttered, already painfully aware that she was losing this argument. It was at times like this that her mother and sister seemed to gang up and work together to make her feel as if she was an outsider, and she was already starting to feel hot and sweaty at the thought of being looked down upon yet again.

"Okay, Ruth," her mother said after a moment with a weary sigh, "why don't you go to the kitchen and get some juice or something?"

"But -"

"Please, Ruth."

Obediently, Ruth turned and headed to the door, but not without glancing back at Charlotte and flashing a self-satisfied smile that made it clear she felt extremely pleased with herself. Yet again, she'd managed to win the day and leave Charlotte looking like the bad sister.

"So what's this all about?" her mother asked once Ruth was out of the room. Fixing Charlotte with a strict, stern gaze, she waited for an answer. "You're eight years old," she continued eventually, "and yet you still spend your time willfully disobeying my rules and going on about some kind of ridiculous fantasy -"

"There's a witch in the cave," Charlotte whined, with tears rolling down her cheeks. "There *is*! Just because you haven't seen her, doesn't mean she's not there!"

"And *you've* seen her, have you?"

Charlotte paused. "Not really."

"Then how do you know she's there?"

"I've heard her," Charlotte continued, aware that she was losing the argument. "I've dreamed about her."

"And do you think dreams are real?"

Charlotte took a deep breath. She hated the way she always started crying when she was being told off. She felt that her more adventurous side had abandoned her, leaving her timid side to face the music. She tried to say something, but her voice was filled with tears and she knew there was nothing she could say or do to change her mother's mind.

"I give up," her mother said after a moment. "If you want to live in a childish fantasy world filled with stupidity, then by all means, go ahead. You'll regret it one day, my girl, but by then it'll be too late. Do you understand? You're supposed to keep moving forward in life, but I can't stop you if you want to go backward, Charlotte. There's only so much I can do to save you from yourself, and I can't keep wearing myself out, trying to make you change." She sighed. "I already have so much on my plate without your father, and I just can't handle any more of this silly behavior."

Charlotte closed her eyes, trying in vain to stop the tears from escaping. She suddenly felt completely exposed and dumb, as if her mother's words were stripping away the very last of her armor. Her mother always had a way of making her feel dumb, and once again it was working. Wiping her face, she finally opened her eyes and realized that her mother was staring at her from the other side of the room.

"I'm sorry," Charlotte sobbed, her bottom lip wobbling. "I just -"

"Sorry doesn't cut it," her mother replied. "Not this time. If you want to live in a fantasy world where a witch lives in a cave at the bottom of the garden, I can't stop you. Just don't blame me when you finally realize that you've made a horrible mistake. And when your sister is living a full and happy live as a grown-up and you're emotionally stunted, don't expect me to apologize for being a horrible mother, because God knows I've tried to help you." She paused. "Go to your room, Charlotte. I'm sick of the sight of you for today. I'll call you down when it's time for dinner."

"Can I eat in my room?" Charlotte asked.

"If you like," her mother replied. "I don't care."

After pausing for a moment, Charlotte turned and ran through to the hallway before making her way upstairs as fast as possible and finally bounding into her room, pushing the door shut and collapsing in a heap of tears onto the bed. She hated herself for crying, and she felt as if Ettolrahc must be completely disappointed. Rolling onto her back, barely able to see a thing through the tears that filled her eyes, she stared at the ceiling and tried to find her adventurous half. All she felt, however, were the wails and cries of her timid half, and no matter how long she waited and how hard she looked, it was as if her adventurous half - by far her *best* half - had deserted her completely, no doubt disgusted by her inability to stop crying.

"Come back," she whispered through the tears. "Please, I'm sorry, come back."

She waited, but even though time passed and the room became darker as the afternoon sun began to dip in the sky, no-one came. Although she turned and looked at her shadow, she soon realized that the only movement came from the rise and fall of her own chest as she breathed; Ettolrahc wasn't playing or dancing or doing anything at all. Dry-eyed, Charlotte turned and stared at the ceiling and realized that there was only one voice in her head.

It was as if, disgusted by Charlotte's tears, Ettolrahc had vanished entirely.

Today

"You wind her up on purpose," Tony said as he chopped a cucumber for the salad. Glancing over at Charlotte, he smiled for a moment before looking back down at the chopping board. "You know all the right buttons to push."

"She's my sister," Charlotte replied, taking a lettuce leaf from the bowl and nibbling the end. "We invented each other's buttons." She paused for a moment, feeling a sudden sensation of concern, as if a shadow had passed momentarily over her heart. Blinking a couple of times, she realized that the sensation had faded just as quickly as it had arrived. "Anyway," she added, "she likes it, or why would she invite me to come and visit every fucking weekend?"

"True," Tony admitted.

"Then again," Charlotte continued, "the invitations have increased tenfold since you-know-who came to live with you. I know Ruth likes to have me as a buffer against Mum, but I still think it's more than that. I think she likes being pissed off at me. It's her only hobby. Believe me, Tony, my sister is a messed-up woman. I guess someone should've warned you before you married her, huh?"

"I'd figured it out by the end of my first date with her," he said with a smile.

"I wouldn't let her hear you say that," Charlotte muttered, liking this slightly spiky side of Tony's personality. He always seemed so put-upon and obedient, slavishly acceding to Ruth's every whim while working long hours to keep the family's finances buoyant, but good old Tony was capable of a few sneaky comments here and there. Charlotte was starting to think that she saw a side of him that Ruth never even suspected. Tony was a man who wore jumpers, and there usually seemed to be little more to his personality than the question of what color jumper he happened to be wearing on any given day. Deep down, though, he seemed to have little flashes of personality.

Looking out the window for a moment, Tony narrowed his eyes a little. "Where's Sophie?" he asked suddenly.

"Playing."

"Where?"

"Dunno," Charlotte said with a shrug. "Just... playing?"

"She's not on the lawn," he replied.

"Down by the river?" She turned and followed his gaze, and although she couldn't see her niece anywhere, she was quite certain that she couldn't have gone very far.

"Huh," Tony muttered, before glancing to her. "Does Ruth know?"

"My overprotective sister?" Charlotte paused. "God knows. Doesn't she have some kind of alarm that goes off whenever Sophie's more than ten feet away?"

"Don't give her ideas."

"Don't worry so much," Charlotte replied with a sigh. "You're as bad as Ruth sometimes. Sophie's not an idiot. She won't..." She paused for a moment. "She's smarter than I was at her age," she continued eventually, "if that's what you're worried about." She watched as Tony continued to make the salad. "Ruth referred to me as the special one again," she added eventually. "Is that my new nickname?"

Tony smiled.

"*Is* it?"

"She's not a bitch, you know," Tony said after a moment. "She's got a good heart. Things just sometimes come out a little wrong, that's all. All she cares about is Sophie. That girl is her world. Sometimes I think we should have had some more children, though, just to ease the pressure on Sophie a little."

"And you think that obsession is healthy?" Charlotte asked, picking up the cucumber stump.

"Do you want to know Ruth's approach to being a mother?" Tony replied, putting the knife down and turning to her. "Whenever she's not sure what to do," he continued, "she just tries to imagine what *your* mother would have done in that situation, and then she does the exact opposite. A complete one hundred and eighty degree march the other way."

"Sounds sensible," Charlotte said, before looking up at the ceiling as she heard a chair leg shifting in one of the rooms upstairs. "Mum was never much good at anything," she added, "apart from drinking, shrieking and going to church. We both recognized her deficiencies when we were younger, but maybe Ruth twigged a little sooner."

"She blames her, you know," Tony replied.

"For what?"

"For what happened to you." He paused, as slow, shuffling footsteps made their way across the bedroom floor directly above the kitchen. "Ruth thinks it all boils down to Helen being inattentive and disorganized, and believe me, when the red wine has been flowing of an evening, she's not shy about voicing her opinion loudly, broadcasting it to the whole house."

"Seriously?"

He nodded. "She ends up strutting around the sofa, lecturing the rest of us about how *awful* life was in this place back when you were children. She doesn't even notice half the time that your mother's nodded off. She just keeps on ranting, gesticulating wildly with her hands as if she's on-stage at the Old Vic. Maybe you'll get a glimpse of it tonight, if you're really lucky."

"Jesus," Charlotte muttered, already starting to tense up now that she knew her mother was coming down to join them. "I had no idea that things were so bad."

"Many's the argument that's raged into the wee small hours," Tony continued. "I think she deliberately doesn't do it when you're here, but on those weekends when you don't come to visit, all hell usually breaks loose. Ruth's got a real temper when she drinks, and she lays into your mother with a kind of ferocity that can be really shocking. I usually have to gently persuade her to come up to bed. Pour a few gins down her throat, that sort of thing, then settle her in, wait until she's passed out, come down, escort your mother to her room, check on Sophie, and then finally, do you know what I do?"

"Shoot yourself in the head?"

"I come down to the empty living room," he continued with a faint smile, "and I pour myself a whiskey, just one, and I drink it alone, in silence. Nothing could be sweeter."

"I can understand Ruth bashing Mum, though," Charlotte pointed out, glancing at the door to the hallway as she heard her mother making her way down the stairs. "Christ," she muttered, "here comes Lady Macbeth, right on cue."

"Where's Sophie?" her mother called out, her voice old and frail but filled with indignation. "Sophie? Where are you, sweetheart? Granny's got something for you!"

"She's outside playing," Charlotte replied, taking a frustrated bite of an asparagus spear.

"Where? Where's she playing?"

"Outside."

"Where outside?" As she reached the bottom of the stairs and shuffled into view, supported by her walking frame, Helen glared at her daughter. "Is someone keeping an eye on her?"

"Yes, Mum," Charlotte replied.

"Who?"

"God."

Sighing, her mother pushed her walking frame to the kitchen table and, with a series of pained gasps, lowered herself into a seat. "It's okay," she muttered eventually, "don't try to help me. It's good for me to battle on alone. Your father would be shocked, though. He'd wonder what kind of a daughter we'd raised, that she doesn't even come and offer her mother a little assistance." Reaching down, she felt her swollen ankles. "Oh, the pain," she said quietly, but just loud enough to be heard. "Sometimes I don't know what I'm going to do."

"I know what you're gonna do," Charlotte whispered under her breath. "You're gonna bitch and -"

"Lunch should be ready soon," Tony said, interrupting her.

"The pain," her mother continued, clearly determined to discuss her health. "It's so bad today."

With a knowing smile, Tony grabbed the sherry bottle from nearby and placed it on the kitchen table. "Would you like a drink, Helen?" he asked, already heading over to get a glass from the cabinet.

"Do you think it might help with my ankles?" the old woman asked innocently, her milky eyes already fixed on the bottle.

"I think it might," Tony replied with well-rehearsed sincerity. It was a routine that they went through every day, as Helen sought to make it clear that she wasn't drinking out of *choice*, but because she required the medicinal effects of a glass of sherry. Several glasses, in fact, and she was usually pretty wasted by the end of lunch. Everyone in the house was happy with this arrangement.

"Go on, then," she said, her frail, shaking hands gripping the bottle and removing the lid before she poured herself a glassful that went all the way to the rim. "I'll try it and see if it helps. You never know, do you, until you give something a whirl?"

"Careful you don't pickle yourself," Charlotte muttered.

"What's that?" her mother asked as she took a sip. "Oh, that's good sherry," she added, acting as if the taste was unfamiliar. Sliding the bottle closer, she examined it closely, as if she'd never seen such a thing before. "Very good indeed. Where did you get this from, Anthony?"

"The same place he gets it from every week," Charlotte whispered. "Your regular fucking supplier."

"They have it in the supermarket," Tony replied, barely able to keep from smiling. "I can get some more if you like it, Helen."

"Oh, not on my account," she replied a little haughtily. "I just thought it might help with my ankles, that's all. They've been so swollen lately, I can barely even sleep at night." Wincing at the pain, she reached down and rubbed the swellings again, as if somehow she thought a little pressure might help. "I'm lucky not to be bedridden," she added. "Dr. Jasper gave me some pills, but I don't know if they do anything. Nothing seems to change much, but then maybe they'd be even worse without the pills. It's so hard to know, and that bloody doctor, I think he's from India, and as much as I want to trust him, I find it terribly difficult. Not because of race, you understand, but because of culture."

"Is she getting worse?" Charlotte whispered to her brother-in-law with a smile.

"Hello," Tony muttered, staring out the window, "someone's on the prowl."

Following his gaze, Charlotte watched as Ruth stood by the river with her hands on her hips, as if she was pissed off about something. "God forbid that Sophie should be allowed to play alone for more than a few minutes," Charlotte muttered.

"She's just worried that -" Tony started to say, before catching himself at the last minute.

"That Sophie might fall down the same rabbit-hole that I fell down?" Charlotte asked with an amused smile.

"She's hardly the first over-protective parent in the world," Tony replied. "They've been around since time began, and I dare say they'll be around long after we're all gone. Every parent fusses over their child."

"*Almost* every parent," Charlotte replied, glancing back at her mother as the old woman's trembling hands refilled her sherry glass. "Some just muddle through and then expect to be treated like parent of the fucking year even though they barely even broke a sweat."

"Ruth's a good mother," Tony continued. "I know I joke about her sometimes, but I shouldn't. If every child had a mother as caring and kind, the world would be a much better place. Maybe she goes overboard from time to time, but the benefits outweigh the downsides every time, you know." He added the last of the tomatoes to the salad. "She went through hell when you were missing, you know," he continued. "She was just at the age to be able to really understand it. She doesn't talk about it much, but I know it's on her mind. Try not to give her a hard time."

"She's a rubbish sister," Charlotte replied, "but maybe she'd have been a useful mother."

Looking out the window, Tony seemed distracted for a moment.

"Uh-oh," he said eventually, his face filled with weary concern, "looks like she's really on the warpath about something."

"What's wrong this time?" Charlotte asked, watching as Ruth hurried across the lawn, making straight for the house. There was something faintly comic about the way Ruth always strutted around when she was angry, and she had a well-worn look of righteous indignation on her face, the same look that usually prompted Charlotte to burst out laughing. Today, however, something was holding back the laughter, and Charlotte felt instead as if maybe there was reason to be concerned after all. Something just felt wrong.

"Hang on," Tony said with weary resignation, removing his apron and hurrying to the back door. "Let's see what fire needs fighting this time."

"I can't find her!" Ruth said, clearly alarmed as she reached the house. "It's Sophie! I can't find her anywhere!"

"She's playing by the river," Charlotte replied matter-of-factly, trying as much to convince herself as to calm her sister.

"I've just *been* down there," Ruth said, filled with panic as she hurried through the door and grabbed Tony's arm. "Come on, we have to find her. There's no sign of her anywhere, and you know how I feel when she wanders off."

"I'm sure she's just having a bit of fun," Tony replied, glancing back at Charlotte with a worried look in his eyes. "Come on, we'll go and see what she's doing. She probably just got distracted by something. I'm pretty sure there's a family of stoats down by the oak trees. It wouldn't surprise me if

Sophie's down there right now, tormenting the poor things."

"She knows not to go out of sight," Ruth continued, leading Tony across the grass. "How many times have I drilled it into her? She *knows* the rules. Is she doing this deliberately? I swear to God, sometimes I think she wants to give me a heart attack!" She kept talking, her words running breathlessly into one another, as she and Tony got further and further from the house. Eventually they were out of Charlotte's earshot, although Ruth's mouth could still be seen running at a thousand miles an hour, peppering her husband with fears and concerns.

Charlotte paused for a moment, feeling the faintest whisper of recognition cross her mind before she turned to see her mother pouring another glass of sherry. "Deja vu?" she said after a moment, trying to smile but unable to feel completely comfortable suddenly, as if some unseen weight had landed on her shoulders. Was this what it had been like, she wondered, when she'd disappeared all those years ago? "Hey, Mum?" she asked, glancing over her shoulder. "Deja vu all over again, huh?"

"What's that?" her mother asked testily.

"Is this how it was with me?" Charlotte asked.

"How what was?"

"Never mind," Charlotte replied with a sigh, before wandering over to the door. Staring out at the garden, she saw Ruth and Tony down by the river, calling out for Sophie. Although she wanted to laugh the whole thing off and assume that the girl was just playing hide-and-seek, Charlotte couldn't ignore the sliver of doubt in her heart, or the voice in the back of her mind that was taunting her over and over again with the possibility that somehow, impossibly, it was all happening again. Exactly as it had happened twenty years ago.

Twenty years ago

By the time morning came, Charlotte was woken by the same stomach cramps that she'd felt the day before. The pain wasn't enough to cause her to cry out, but it put a frown on her face and left her curled up on her side, with one hand resting on her belly while she waited for the sensation to pass.

She could hear her mother pottering about in the kitchen downstairs, and a few minutes later she heard her sister running excitedly past the bedroom door. The smell of breakfast was wafting up the stairs, but Charlotte stayed exactly where she was. With the dull, dark pain still floating in her stomach, she didn't feel like eating, and she wasn't even sure if she *was* allowed to go downstairs. In a way, it felt as if Ruth and her mother had formed a little gang, deliberately excluding Charlotte because of her insubordination. As if to prove the point, Charlotte soon heard their muffled voices from the room below, talking happily to one another.

Finally, Charlotte decided she had no choice but to get out of bed. She sat up, which made the pain feel a little worse for a moment before seemingly clearing whatever knot was causing the problem. She took a deep breath, still able to feel the pain's echo, but at least it seemed to be slowly passing. As she shifted toward the edge of the bed, however, she felt something wet against her leg. Moving to one side, she looked down, fearing that she might have wet herself, but instead she saw a few small spots of blood. After staring at the red stain for a moment, she glanced over at her discarded clothes from the night before, and to her horror she saw that there was some old, dried blood in her underwear. With her heart racing, she realized that the blood could only mean one thing.

***

"It happens to every woman eventually," her mother said half an hour later, as they sat alone at the kitchen table. "It's just happening to you a little earlier than most girls."

Charlotte shifted uncomfortably in her seat. Her sister Ruth had been banished to play in the garden, somewhat against her will, and this gave Charlotte a mild degree of satisfaction. Ruth was older, and yet it seemed that her mother had sought to exclude her from this particular conversation. Still, the things her mother was saying made no sense to Charlotte; it seemed completely fantastical that her body might not only have decided to shed part of itself, but also that it might be planning to do the same thing every month from now on. It sounded like some kind of weird fairytale.

"It's a good thing," her mother continued with a faint smile. "The discomfort is a part of the process. For some women it can be quite debilitating, for others it's little more than an annoyance. You'll have to wait and see how it goes with you, but if it's any consolation, none of the women in your family have a history of difficult periods." She paused, as if she wasn't sure what to say. "Do you have any questions, Charlotte? Don't be shy. Just tell me what you're thinking about, and I'll try to answer as truthfully and helpfully as possible."

Charlotte paused. "But are you *sure* I'm not dying?" she asked eventually.

"One hundred per cent certain."

"But blood means something's dying," Charlotte continued.

"Or living," her mother pointed out. "Blood means life as well."

Charlotte frowned. "Does Ruth have this?"

"Not yet," her mother replied, "but she will, one day soon. She's older than you, so one would have thought that she'd be affected first, but there's really no strict order to these things. It's quite unusual for it to strike a girl as young as eight, although there are exceptional cases."

"So it might *not* be what you say it is?" Charlotte asked, as she felt a twist of pain pass briefly through her belly once again. "You might be wrong?"

"I'm not wrong."

"But you -"

"I'm not wrong," her mother said again, more firmly this time. "Charlotte, there's no reason to be scared about growing up." She paused. "Is this what your behavior has been about recently? Have you been feeling yourself growing up, and it's been scaring you? If that's the problem, you really have nothing to worry about. You're starting to become a woman, and that means you're at the start of a wonderful adventure that's going to take you to lots of great places. It also means that you have to be careful with your decisions, because you're going to reach the point soon where those decisions start to define not only how your day turns out, but how your life develops." She paused again. "Do you understand, Charlotte?"

Charlotte stared at her mother, wondering why she was lying. For Charlotte, all this talk of biological changes and physical maturity and becoming a woman... it was all rubbish, and she felt that her mother was insulting her intelligence. No, the blood in the bed and in her underwear could only mean one thing: Ettolrahc had died, had curled up inside her and passed away, and those spots of blood were the only visible traces of this tragedy that had taken place inside her body. Still, she couldn't help clinging to the hope that maybe Ettolrahc wasn't quite dead, but merely wounded, in which case she could potentially be revived if Charlotte could think of something that might help.

Turning to look out the window, she thought of something. She smiled.

"So we'll look into a few other things we need to do for you," her mother said eventually, "and I'll show you how to use certain products that a woman must get to grips with. I hope, also, that you might stop talking about various infantile matters that have been consuming your time lately. All this talk of witches down at the bottom of the garden or living in a cave, Charlotte... It's childish nonsense, and it has to end. People are going to laugh at you and question your intelligence if you persist with such rubbish." She waited for a reply. "Charlotte?"

Slowly, filled with a great plan but aware that she had to keep it to herself, Charlotte turned to face her mother.

"Will you abandon all these childish thoughts about witches and suchlike?" her mother continued. "Will you try to be more grown up, now that your body has shown that it's starting to mature?"

Charlotte nodded.

"Thank you," her mother said with a smile. "You know, in a strange way, this has all happened at a very opportune moment. If you can approach the changes with intelligence, I think the whole thing could be the making of you."

Charlotte smiled. She was lying, of course, but she also knew that grown-ups tended to lie. A lot. Therefore, she was 'growing up' by lying, which meant keeping her thoughts and activities a secret from her mother. If other people wanted to believe strange stories about girls' bodies shedding linings from inside, Charlotte felt that this was entirely up to them and she had no interest in proving them wrong. She, however, was going to focus on her own beliefs, which she felt made far more sense. Besides, she knew her body better than anyone else. It was fine and dandy for her mother to suddenly start making a bunch of absurd claims, but Charlotte felt that it couldn't be a coincidence that the blood had arrive the morning after she'd felt Ettolrahc disappear.

"Ruth will have a lot of questions," her mother added. "If it gets too much for you, tell her to come and ask me, okay?"

Charlotte nodded.

"Maybe you'd like to go outside and play now?"

Getting up from the chair, Charlotte walked carefully over to the back door. She wanted to run, but she knew she had to be more careful and at least pretend that she'd listened to her mother's words. As she reached the door and pulled it open, she glanced back at her mother and saw that she seemed satisfied and confident, as if she felt that she'd 'fixed' her troublesome, wayward daughter. Charlotte hated letting her think that she'd won, but she figured that this was only a battle, and that the more important thing was to focus on the overall war.

Confident that she'd be proved right eventually, Charlotte headed outside into the bright sunny day. As she spotted Ruth playing in the grass, she suddenly felt as if she'd somehow overtaken her sister. She'd go and join in the game for a while, of course, but her participation would be a charade to cover up her true plans.

In this way, at least, Charlotte felt that maybe she *had* become a little more grown-up after all.

Today

"Sophie!" Ruth shouted, cupping her hands around her mouth as she stood on the riverbank. "Sophie! Where are you?"

As she caught up to her sister and brother-in-law, Charlotte felt a pang of fear in her chest. She kept trying to tell herself not to be scared, that everything would be okay, but deep down there was a long-dormant kernel of panic starting to sprout again. It seemed utterly impossible that Sophie could have come to any harm, especially down here by the river of all places, but every time she reassured her sister that things would be okay, Charlotte heard a nagging voice at the back of her head that told her maybe she was wrong.

"Jesus Christ," Ruth said as she hurried along the path, "where the hell is she?"

"I'm sure she's around here somewhere," Tony said, clearly forcing himself to stay calm even though his eyes betrayed the same doubts and fears that Charlotte was feeling. "She's a sensible girl, Ruth -"

"It's not about being sensible," Ruth replied firmly, "it's about being safe!" She hurried a little further along the riverbank, before stopping again and pausing, as if she was waiting for a hint of movement. "Sophie!" she shouted at the top of her voice. "It's Mummy! I need you to come back immediately!"

"You're not in any trouble!" Tony shouted, hurrying after his wife. "We just want to make sure you're okay!"

Walking after them, Charlotte couldn't help but keep glancing down at the river, as if she expected to see a limp little body go floating past. Something deep inside was already telling her that there was a problem, and she knew that Sophie was at heart a very timid and smart girl who'd never disappear like this on purpose. There was just no way that the events of twenty years ago could be playing out all over again. No family could be so unlucky.

"She's only been gone for a few minutes," Tony said, putting a hand on Ruth's shoulder. "Let's not panic just yet, eh?"

"And when do you think we *should* panic?" Ruth asked. "After six minutes? Seven? An hour? A day?" She glanced back at Charlotte. "A year?"

"Don't overreact," Charlotte muttered, although she immediately knew that she'd chosen the wrong words.

"Don't overreact?" Ruth replied, her voice filled with scorn. "Is that the best advice you can offer right now?"

"Fine," Charlotte said. "Overreact. Go for it!"

Ruth stared at her for a moment, unable to disguise her anger, before turning and continuing her way along the riverbank, pulling free of Tony in the process. She was clearly getting worked up into a tighter and tighter ball of energy, and it was only a matter of time before she'd explode. Charlotte knew her sister too well, and she knew that even without any cause, Ruth was capable of causing a real scene; with Sophie missing, it was clear that there'd be no limits to the woman's anger.

"She's just worried," Tony said.

Charlotte nodded.

"She thinks -"

"I know what she thinks," Charlotte replied.

"It's just that -"

"I know!" Charlotte insisted, keen to avoid talking about the specifics. "I know exactly what she's thinking. You don't need to tell me. I'm thinking it too. I'm sure we're all thinking it."

"It's nonsense, of course," Tony continued, "but Sophie's eight, the same age as you when -"

"I know!" Charlotte said firmly, before realizing that she was letting her concern show. "Come on, it can't be happening again. That's a ludicrous idea! She's going to come running out of some bush somewhere any moment, probably covered in mud, with some crazy story about where she's been, and then... and then Ruth'll blow a gasket and act like something awful's happened, and then there'll be lots of drama and things'll start to settle down." She paused, hoping to God that she was right. "Sophie's fine," she added.

"Of course she is," Tony said unconvincingly. "She's a smart girl."

"Exactly," Charlotte replied. "I mean, when I went missing, I was dumb. Really fucking dumb. Believe me, even for an eight-year-old, I was pretty bone-headed. Sophie's not like that. The kid's smart and she knows what she's doing. She can look after herself."

"Sophie!" Ruth shouted up ahead, sounding increasingly desperate. "Sophie, where are you?"

"She must be able to hear us," Tony muttered. "You're right, she's smart, and she's not deaf either. She must be doing this on purpose. She could have -" He stopped suddenly. "Oh fuck," he said after a moment. "Please, Ruth, don't take this too far."

It was too late. Up ahead, Ruth had finally reached the entrance to the cave. Back when she and Charlotte were children, the cave was a forbidden place, and they were told over and over again by their parents to never, ever go into the darkness. Of course, while Ruth had been obedient and well-behaved, Charlotte had eventually rebelled against such strict instructions, and when she was exactly Sophie's age, she went blundering in there. The shadow of that afternoon's misadventure had been hanging over the family ever since, and now Ruth was standing at the entrance, staring into the darkness.

"She's not in there!" Tony said as he caught up to her. "Ruth, there's no way she'd be in there!"

"How do you know?" she asked, her voice thick with tension.

"Why the hell would she do something so stupid?" he continued. "We've told her over and over not to go in there."

"So?" Ruth replied, still staring into the cave. "Maybe she decided to go in anyway, just to spite us."

"Look," Tony pointed out, "the grass around the entrance hasn't been disturbed or tramped down. There's no way she's been this way. She's probably back up at the house by now, wondering where we all are."

"You don't know that," Ruth said. "What if..." Pausing for a moment, she finally turned to look back at Charlotte. "What if she's done the same thing you did all those years ago?"

"There's no way," Charlotte replied. "Don't be fucking stupid, Ruth. You're -"

"Don't tell me I'm overreacting!" Ruth shouted back at her. "You don't have children, Charlotte, so you don't know what it's like! You don't have a clue! You're barren, remember? You probably don't even have the capability to understand how a mother feels about her child!"

Charlotte held her hands up in mock surrender. "I'm sure she's fine," she said, trying to make herself believe her own empty rhetoric, and ignoring the desire to punch her sister's lights out. "Whatever she's doing -"

"You were egging her on," Ruth continued, warming to her theme. "Back there in the garden, you were filling her mind with all sorts of nonsense, about monsters in the basement and horrible, deformed mutant children, and now look where it's got us! You've got her thinking about that kind of thing -"

"You mean she's actually got a mind of her own," Charlotte snapped back at her, annoyed that once again she was being blamed for the family's problems.

"Calm down," Tony said quietly. "Charlotte's just trying to help -"

"No!" Ruth said firmly, pushing her husband away as she approached her sister. "You need to hear this, Charlotte. You filled my daughter's head with all sorts of rubbish, and now she's run off somewhere! She could be hurt! She could be dying!" As her eyes filled with tears, Ruth waited for an answer. "She's eight years old, Charlotte! Eight! She's exactly the same age that you were when you disappeared!"

"She hasn't disappeared," Charlotte replied, stunned by the force of Ruth's anger. "She's just... gone... somewhere. It's perfectly normal for a little girl to want to -"

"How would you know what's normal?" Ruth spit back at her, before turning and picking her way through the long grass that led into the cave.

"Hold on!" Tony called, hurrying after her. "Ruth, you can't go in there! Sophie hasn't been this way! You're panicking over nothing!" He waited for Ruth to reply, but she was forcing her way forward. "Ruth, seriously," he continued, "you're not thinking straight! Why would Sophie go in there?"

"I'll go back to the house!" Charlotte shouted after them, figuring that there was nothing more for her to be doing down by the river. "I'll see if she's there, and then I'll go and take a look at some of the fields!" She waited for a reply, but her sister and brother-in-law were still bickering as they disappeared into the shadows of the cave. "Fine!" Charlotte shouted. "You two go stumbling around in the dark, and I'll go and actually do something useful that might help us find your daughter!" She waited for a reply. "Great," she muttered, turning and heading back along the riverbank, "at least we all know where we stand!"

She made her way slowly back to the house, constantly turning and looking over her shoulder in case there was any sign of Sophie. Trying to ignore the voice of doubt in the pit of her stomach, she kept insisting to herself that Sophie had merely wandered off, and that there was no way history could repeat itself, not in such a specific and cruel fashion. Nevertheless, with every second that passed, she became more and more worried, until finally she reached the house and breathlessly entered the kitchen, only to find her mother passed out at the table with one outstretched hand resting next to the half-empty bottle of sherry.

"Sophie!" Charlotte shouted, hurrying through to the hallway and calling up the stairs. "Sophie, are you here?"

Silence.

"Sophie!" She waited again, but this time she knew there wasn't going to be a reply. That voice in the back of her mind, insisting that something was wrong, was getting louder and louder, drowning out all of Charlotte's other thoughts. She tried to think of all the places Sophie could be, all the places she could have hidden or fallen, until finally she began to contemplate the one possibility that she'd been trying desperately to ignore: the possibility that somehow, Sophie had ended up in the same place where Charlotte had ended up all those years ago. With trembling hands, she fumbled in her pocket for her cigarettes and lighter.

"This isn't happening," she whispered. "Not again. The world is not this fucking cruel."

Twenty years ago

Having played with Ruth for a few hours, Charlotte had finally managed to slip away. Now she stood alone at the side of the tow-path, facing the cave, and she knew exactly what she had to do.

And why she had to do it.

Placing a hand on her belly, where there was still a faint, fluttering pain, she tried to persuade Ettolrahc to hold on just a little longer. She felt that there must be a chance she could revive that other voice in her head, if only she could prove to it that there was still some point in sticking around. It was quite obvious to Charlotte that the previous day's events had struck a mortal blow to Ettolrahc, and that her timidity in the face of her mother and sister had made her adventurous side give up on her entirely. Each tear that flowed down Charlotte's face had probably seemed like a dagger to Ettolrahc, cutting her again and again until she was struck down by death itself. There must have been a lot of blood, even if only a few specks had leaked out of Charlotte's body.

"It's okay," Charlotte whispered, staring at the cave's dark entrance. "I'll show you." It felt silly to talk to herself, but she felt that she had to give some kind of verbal encouragement to Ettolrahc. "We'll be brave together," she added, "and I'll show you that I'm not weak."

Despite these words, however, she felt desperately scared. The cave had always been considered out of bounds, and Charlotte's mother had warned her over and over again to never go inside. Still, in recent days, an argument of unprecedented ferocity had been raging inside Charlotte's head. Ettolrahc had wanted to go exploring, to plunge into the darkness and see what might be found, whereas Charlotte had wanted to just play the way they always played on a warm summer's day. Eventually, Charlotte had won out, but in doing so she seemed to have struck a mortal blow to Ettolrahc. There had been a little unease between the two voices in her head, of course, but she had never guessed that the result could be blood. As she stood in the mouth of the cave, barefoot and nervous, she tried to ignore her fear, and she allowed only the faintest flicker of doubt to cross her features.

"Okay," Charlotte whispered, aware that there was no point delaying things any longer. "It's time."

Slowly, she started walking forward into the wet cave, her bare feet instantly feeling cold. She was convinced that at any moment, the witch of the cave might leap out and make her presence known, and Charlotte had already managed to conjure up all sorts of horrific visions of how the witch might look;

perhaps she'd be a green-skinned, wart-covered monster with a stove hat; or maybe she'd be an old crone, with straggly long hair and rounded, swollen joints; worst of all, she might look like a normal woman, her power hiding deeper beneath the surface and behind a pair of calm, seductive eyes. Charlotte wanted to be ready for any eventuality, yet she also believed that the witch would probably be capable of surprising her with another form entirely.

Barely a few meters into the cave, Charlotte could hear water running somewhere beneath the rocks upon which she was standing, as a smaller river flowed somewhere in the darkness.

A drop of cold water fell from the wet roof and landed on the back of Charlotte's neck, causing her to take a shocked step back and, in the process, almost knocking her off her balance. She paused for a moment and took a deep breath, almost losing her confidence and bravery. Almost, but not quite. She steeled herself before reaching down and wiping some dirt from the soles of her feet, hoping that cleaner skin might give her a better grip on the wet rocks. As she made her way forward, she could hear drips deeper in the cave, echoing as they hit the water. It was like being in another world entirely, but she kept telling herself not to be scared: after all, at the first sign of trouble, she could just turn and run back out. Escape was always an option, and Ettolrahc wouldn't want her to get hurt.

"Hello?" she called out. The word immediately echoed all around her, as if the witch had caught her voice and shattered it into a million little pieces.

She waited as the echoes died away.

Her belly gave another twist of pain, as if Ettolrahc was stirring. Charlotte felt certain that by proving her bravery, she could bring her old friend back to life and stop the blood. She just needed to keep going.

When she reached the edge of the rocks and looked down into the water, she knew she should turn around. Still, she'd been hoping to find something a little darker and more unusual, something that absolutely, irrevocably belonged to this new underground world, so she clambered up the side of another rock until she was balanced delicately on the top, looking down into shadows that seemed as if they were poised to gobble her up. She wobbled a little, her dirty hands constantly seeking fresh purchase on the rock's dark, wet surface. Using her knees, she turned around and peered further back into the cave. The darkness seemed to go on forever, and she was tempted to think that maybe the cave never ended.

"Hello?" she called out again, starting to feel the cold, damp air on her skin. "My name's Charlotte Abernathy! I'm looking for the witch!" As soon as the words left her mouth, she knew that they sounded stupid and childish, but she still believed that this was the only way she could possibly revive Ettolrahc. Despite the freezing cold of the cave, she hoped that Ettolrahc might suddenly warm her from within.

    Spotting another rocky outcrop nearby, she decided to go a little further. She strengthened her grip with one hand, while reaching out with the other to the next rock, hoping to straddle the two and then make a crossing. The job was delicate, and she knew full well that she had to be careful, but after a moment she was able to bridge the two rocks. Maneuvering her knees, she tried to swing one leg out to the other rock, but she found the distance to be a little further than she'd imagined. Pausing for a moment, she realized that she was in a difficult position, and that going backward would be no easier than going forward. Taking another deep breath, she used the tips of her fingers to grip the next rock before reaching over with her other hand. She wasn't sure whether to jump or whether to retreat, but she figured that maybe the best option would be just to -

    And that's when her knee slipped against the first rock, instantly sending her tumbling down into the darkness below. Within just a couple of seconds, the only sound was the continued dripping of water from the roof of the cave, and it was as if Charlotte had never been there at all.

Part Two

Sinking

Twenty years ago

"Mummy!" Charlotte shouted, her voice filled with pain and fear and tears. "Mummy, help me! Please!"

She waited, gulping at the air as she tried to stay calm. The pain from her snapped ankle had become so intense and overpowering, she could barely even think. All she knew was that she was cold and alone down in the darkness of the cave, and she couldn't understand why her mother was taking so long to find her. Surely she must know? Surely she must have heard her cries?

Reaching down, she fumbled in the pitch darkness as she ran her fingers down her leg until she reached the site of the immense pain. The tips of her fingers ran against torn, bloodied skin, and suddenly she felt a sharp jolt of pain as her fingertips touched something hard and jagged. A piece of bone was jutting out the side of her ankle.

"Mummy," she whimpered for a moment, before realizing that whimpering wouldn't be enough. She needed to be loud. "Mummy!" she screamed at the top of her voice. "Mummy! Help me!"

Today

"And the last time you saw Sophie, was... what time exactly?"

Standing in the kitchen, the two police officers had cautious, sympathetic looks on their faces, which Charlotte figured they must have had drummed into them on some kind of sensitivity training course. They were doing a very good job of pretending to be taking the whole situation seriously, even though Charlotte was convinced that they were probably, secretly, finding it hard to deal with Ruth's histrionics. It had only been three hours since Sophie had gone down to play by the river, and Charlotte felt that it had been an overreaction to call the police. Then again, she was also very much aware that her sense of perspective was probably warped.

"I've told you this a thousand times already," Ruth said, fiddling with a tissue as she sat, red-eyed and tear-stained, at the kitchen table. She was filled with a kind of calmness that seemed poised to explode at any moment. "It was lunchtime. My husband was in here making a salad..." She paused for a moment. "My sister, as usual, was flitting about the place, and my mother, as usual, was drinking. It was about half twelve, and Sophie said she was going to go and play." Her voice began to tremble for a moment. "That's all she wanted to do," she continued, with tears rolling down her cheeks. "She wanted to play..."

"And how long was it before you noticed she was missing?" the male police officer asked, writing something in his notebook.

"About ten minutes," Ruth replied, taking a deep breath as she tore pieces off the tissue. "It can't have been more than that. I'm not a bad mother. I just let her play for a few minutes, and then I looked down toward the river, and there was no sign of her."

"I noticed she wasn't there a few minutes earlier," Charlotte added.

"You did *what*?" Ruth asked, turning to her sister with a shocked look on her face.

"Just a couple of minutes earlier," Charlotte continued hesitantly, wondering if it had been strictly necessary to make such an admission. "I didn't think anything of it at the time -"

"You didn't think anything *of* it?" Ruth asked, the anger building in her voice once again. "Are you fucking kidding me? My daughter disappeared from view and you thought there was no reason to *mention* it?"

"It wasn't just me," Charlotte replied, looking over at Tony. "You looked out the window too, remember? You saw she wasn't there!"

Ruth turned to her husband, and it was clear that she was quickly forming the opinion that everyone else was to blame for Sophie's disappearance.

"I might have glanced over," Tony said hesitantly, "but I wasn't exactly looking for her."

"Let's all stay calm," said the female police officer, turning to Charlotte. "When you say a couple of minutes -"

"Two, tops," Charlotte replied. "I just looked out the window and noticed I couldn't see Sophie, but I figured she was just out of sight. You know, behind a tree or something. Doing kid stuff."

"Well that's alright then," Ruth said, fixing her sister with a look of pure hatred. "Maybe that's still where she is, huh? Behind a fucking tree?"

"Ninety per cent of the time," the male officer said, interrupting what was threatening to turn into a full-blown tirade, "children are found very quickly once we've been called in. It's simply a matter of making sure that people in the area are aware of the need to keep an eye out. I want to make it very clear to you that the odds of someone snatching your daughter are very small. Most likely, she's simply wandered off somewhere -"

"Or she's hurt," Ruth interjected.

"We're not ruling anything out," the male officer replied.

"I'm afraid our family doesn't have a very good track record when it comes to missing children," Ruth said bitterly, staring at Charlotte with an expression that made her anger very visible. "Ask my sister."

"I'm sorry?" the officer replied.

"Ask her," Ruth continued, her words dripping with disdain.

Charlotte felt her heart sink as everyone in the room turned to her. She'd known that the subject would have to come up eventually, but she'd been hoping to put it off for as long as possible. Whenever she had to talk about her past, she always felt as if she was being accused of some terrible crime.

"It was twenty years ago," she said with a sigh. "It's really not going to be relevant."

"What happened?" the female officer asked.

"It doesn't matter..."

"Please," the male officer said, "let us be the judge of that. Just tell us what happened to you."

"I was eight years old," Charlotte replied, figuring that there was no point delaying the inevitable. "I was playing in the garden with my sister, with Ruth, and..." She paused for a moment, trying to think back to that long-ago day before hitting the mental wall that always prevented her from remembering it properly. "I don't really remember it very well," she continued, "but apparently I went off by myself, down to the river, and I ended up going into this small cave up near the bridge, and..."

"And she disappeared," Ruth said, as if the words sickened her. "To cut a long story short."

"For how long?" the male officer asked.

Charlotte and Ruth exchanged a worried glance.

"A day?" the female officer asked. "A couple of days?"

"A year," Charlotte said eventually, before clearing her throat nervously. "There was an extensive search. I'm sure you have records in your system somewhere. Police dogs, helicopters, national appeals, you name it. Everyone looked for me, but eventually, after a few weeks, the media moved on and..." She paused again. "They could never work out of I'd had an accident, or been snatched or whatever, but after a year they'd pretty much given up on the idea that I'd ever be found -"

"That's not true," Ruth said firmly.

"Yeah," Charlotte replied, "it kind of is. Ask Mum. And then, exactly a year later to the day, I came wandering up to the house from the bottom of the garden, from near the river. No memory, no recollection of where I'd been or anything. I was just... back!"

"Maybe the witch took you," Ruth muttered with clear disdain.

"There must have been an investigation," the male officer said, clearly taken aback by the tale.

Charlotte nodded.

"It was all Charlotte's little mystery," Ruth said bitterly. "She always claims she doesn't remember a thing, and that we should all just stop asking where she was. She acts like it doesn't really matter. An eight-year-old girl vanishes for a year, and when she comes back, everyone's supposed to just shrug and get on with their lives."

"I didn't say that it doesn't matter," Charlotte replied, forcing herself to stay calm. "I said that I don't remember what happened."

"And you don't want to find out, either, do you?" Ruth replied.

"Not particularly," Charlotte muttered.

"See?" Ruth said, turning to the police officers. "See what I have to put up with here? What kind of person doesn't even care about what happened to her while she was missing?"

"And you really don't know where you were for a year?" the female officer asked. "That... must be quite a difficult thing for you to get your head around."

Charlotte shrugged.

"She refuses to try psychotherapy," Ruth muttered. "It's like she doesn't want to know the truth. Either that, or she's lying her ass off and she just doesn't want to say."

"This isn't about me," Charlotte continued, determined to get the focus back onto Sophie. "What happened to me is just a coincidence. It's not gonna help anyone find Sophie any quicker, is it?" She paused. "I mean, that's why we're here, right? To find Sophie? Not to rehash everything that happened with me."

"But in both cases," the female officer added, "the missing child was eight years old?"

Charlotte nodded wearily.

"Same age," Ruth said firmly, "same place, same family. Is that really a coincidence?"

"This is some kind of sick joke," Tony said, still staring out the window. "It has to be. Someone's doing this on purpose, to torture us." He paused, before turning to the police officers. "Couldn't that be it? Someone wants to mess with our heads, and they know about what happened before, so they've done this because they want to watch us squirm. There's no other explanation."

"Do you have any enemies?" the male officer asked.

Ruth shook her head.

"Miracle of miracles," Charlotte muttered under her breath.

"The house is very remote," the female officer pointed out. "Where's your nearest neighbor?"

"About four miles away," Ruth replied, her voice trembling. "We've already phoned everyone in the area, but no-one's seen her. They're all going to keep an eye out and search their out-buildings, just in case she turns up." She paused for a moment. "You need to..." Her voice trailed off, and she put her head in her hands, clearly starting to sob. "Divers," she blurted out eventually, taking big gulps of air. "You need to check the river! She might -" Before she could finish, put her head in her hands and began to sob. "You need to check the river," she said eventually, as her tears dripped down onto the kitchen table. "She might have been washed away..."

"We're going to do everything in our power to find your daughter," the male officer said, glancing over at Charlotte for a moment before turning back to Tony, who had hurried over to put an arm around his wife. "I need someone to draw up a list of any places in the area that she might have gone. Parks, buildings, school... any place she might be familiar with. If she's lost, she might head to a familiar location and hope that someone comes to find her. Children sometimes do that if for some reason they're disorientated. If that's the case, we need to get to her before nightfall."

"There are a few places," Tony said. "There's are a couple of parks we go to sometimes, and there's the dog shelter, and -"

"Can you write them down for me, Sir?" the office said, passing him the notebook and a pen. "Anywhere you can think of. It might seem silly, but we have to check every possible location. Would you describe Sophie as being worldly-wise? Do you think she'd be good at looking after herself?"

Charlotte couldn't help but grin at the suggestion.

"She's eight years old," Tony said, as Ruth continued to sob at the table. "How worldly-wise can an eight-year-old girl be?"

"She's smart, though," Charlotte added, hoping to provide a sliver of hope. "She's really smart for her age."

"She knew not to wander off," Tony continued. "We drummed that into her head over and over."

As the discussion continued, Charlotte waited a few minutes before slipping over to the door and heading out into the garden. She'd been feeling suffocated in the house, as if somehow everyone was blaming her for Sophie's disappearance. Standing on the porch and staring down toward the river, she waited for some sign of life; anything that might indicate Sophie's sudden return. Although she fully understood the seriousness of the situation, she hadn't yet given up hope that this was all some kind of huge misunderstanding, in which case Sophie might suddenly come running home, breathless with excitement and completely shocked that anyone was worried about her. That was the best-case scenario, at least.

"This must be very difficult for you," said the female officer, coming out to join her. "I'm sorry, we weren't introduced properly. I'm Eve Locklear. I do a lot of cases like this."

Charlotte nodded, preferring not to shake the woman's outstretched hand.

"I hope you don't mind," Eve continued, "but I'd like to ask you a few questions about the time you went missing."

"It's a pretty simple story," Charlotte muttered. "I went missing, and then a year later I came back. Apparently, anyway."

"Apparently?"

"It was twenty years ago," Charlotte replied, hoping to head off any questions as quickly as possible. "I was a kid, I really don't remember anything. Most of it, I just know from what I've been told."

"But you were away for a year?"

Charlotte nodded again.

"And you don't remember anything at all from that year? Not even a place or a face?"

"Nothing," Charlotte replied. "Before you mention it, my sister was lying. I *did* go and see a psychotherapist. I had several extremely tedious and expensive sessions before I finally figured I'd tried enough and there was no need to put myself through any more of that crap. I wasn't making any progress. Whatever I forgot, it's probably best left undisturbed."

Eve paused. "Were you examined for -"

"Yes!" Charlotte said firmly, keen to cut the question off. "I was poked and prodded once I came back, and generally examined at great length. There was nothing wrong with me, and nothing had been done to me." She sighed. "That's the first thing everyone fucking things."

"But you must be curious about what happened," Eve replied. "If it was me, I'd be going crazy until I got an answer."

"People always say that," Charlotte replied with a sad smile. "People always think I must be traumatized by the whole thing, but the truth is, I've managed to rather successfully compartmentalize things and not think about it too much. I don't know if that makes me lucky or unlucky, or smart or dumb, but it's the truth. I'm not haunted by nightmares, I don't wake up sweating in the middle of the night, I have a perfectly reasonable sex life, I don't use drink or drugs to self-medicate my fears, I just..." She paused, aware once again of a faint tightening sensation in her chest. "I get by. I deal with any doubts I have, and I get on with life. There's no point wading back into the past."

"Still," Eve continued, "a year -"

"Is a very long time," Charlotte said, with a hint of bitterness in her voice, "but the way I see it is that if I'm okay with not knowing, then no good can come of raking up the past. And ultimately it's *my* life, so I figure I'm old enough and stubborn enough to make my own decisions."

"But if something traumatic happened to you -"

"Then it's a good job I don't remember it, huh?" Charlotte replied. "I mean, seriously, isn't that a *great* thing? Shouldn't I be fucking over the moon that my subconscious mind, or whatever, has managed to bury it away? I mean, the whole point of fucking therapy is to help you get over and deal with shit, and I've managed that all by myself. I should be fucking commended and told I'm a genius, not pushed to go and see some quack doctor who might be able to fuck my head up for me." She paused for a moment as she realized that she was probably allowing herself to get too worked up. "I'm fine as I am. I'm not perfect, but I'm not nearly as fucked up as the rest of my family. I guess I just don't have their insatiable desire to go ripping things apart, looking for cracks."

"You must have been affected in some way," Eve replied.

"Nope," Charlotte said, starting to feel as if she needed a cigarette. She decided to hold back, but she knew the siren call would be too strong eventually. "I guess I'm lucky," she added. "I was able to put it all in the past and focus on the future."

"And you were eight years old when it happened?" Eve asked. "Just like Sophie?"

Charlotte nodded.

"And it happened in the exact same place? And in the same way? Down by the river at the bottom of the garden?"

"I guess so," Charlotte replied, immediately tensing as she realized that her own personal explanation, that it was all a coincidence, probably wouldn't wash with everyone. She knew, deep down, that she was probably just trying to deflect questions, but at the same time, she couldn't see how there could possibly be a link. The last thing she wanted was for Sophie's disappearance to be used as an excuse to dig into her own troubles.

"We need to consider every possibility," Eve said after a moment. "Even if -"

"Like what?" Charlotte asked. "That whatever happened to me, has happened to Sophie? In the exact same way? Are you serious? How the fuck would that even work? Whatever happened to me, it was a once in a lifetime, one in a million kind of deal, and there's no way lightning could strike twice. When we find out where Sophie is, which *will* happen, you'll all see that any similarities are just totally superficial."

"You seem a little defensive."

"Of course I'm fucking defensive," Charlotte replied, reaching into her pocket and pulling out a pack of cigarettes and a lighter. She was damn well not going to bother fighting her nicotine craving, not on a day that so far had delivered nothing but a whole load of trouble. "You want one?"

Eve shook her head.

After lighting up, Charlotte took a long drag and held the smoke in her mouth before exhaling slowly. "It's a disgusting habit," she said after a moment, "but it helps." She paused. "Whatever happened to me when I went missing," she continued eventually, "it didn't hurt, and it didn't leave scars, and I've learned to live with it, so..." She took another drag on her cigarette, her eyes fixed on the glistening water of the river a couple of hundred meters away. "It's got nothing to do with whatever's happened to Sophie."

"And what do you think *has* happened to Sophie?" Eve asked.

Charlotte paused. "An accident," she said finally. "The kid's too smart to just go wandering off by herself, and all that talk of her getting abducted is bullshit." She took a deep breath. "She's hurt. Maybe not badly, but enough so that she can't get back home. Maybe she's unconscious, or maybe she just got lost and she's wandering through some field somewhere. My sister was right, though. You need to be checking the river. She might have fallen into the water, in which case she could have been swept downstream."

"There's also that cave," Eve pointed out.

Charlotte shook her head. "There's nothing in there," she said quickly.

"We still need to take a look."

"It's barely even a cave," Charlotte replied, trying not to sound too annoyed. "It doesn't go very far back, and all you'll find is some wet rocks and a damp smell. Everyone acts like it's some kind of fucking mystical place, but it's nothing of the sort. It's just a dank little place with no light and a bunch of wet rocks, and a river dribbling out of a hole."

"An eight-year-old girl isn't very big in the grand scheme of things," Eve pointed out. "There are plenty of place she could be. We have to search each and every one of them, including the cave."

"If you want to waste your time," Charlotte replied, "that's your own business, but there's no way Sophie'd go in there. She's too timid and careful." She paused. "You don't know her. I *do*. You've seen what my sister's like, right? She's the most attentive, coddling mother in the world, and she's made damn sure that Sophie's afraid of her own shadow. It's a miracle she was brave enough to go down to the river by herself, let alone go out of sight for even a fraction of a second. She's great kid, but she's timid as hell."

"Were you the same?" Eve asked. "When you disappeared, I mean. Were you timid and cautious?"

Charlotte paused again, finding the question to be a little personal. "I was a bit of both back then," she replied eventually, not wanting to arouse suspicion. "I had my moments." Stubbing the cigarette out against the side of the house, she tossed the butt to the ground. She wanted to say that Sophie would be okay, to express some kind of meaningless platitude that might somehow make them both feel better for a few minutes, but she couldn't quite bring herself to get the words out. Hearing the sound of Ruth sobbing in the kitchen, she decided that she should probably go back inside and see if she could help. For the first time in years, maybe even the first time ever, she actually felt bad for her sister.

"Sorry," she said to Eve, "I think I'm needed. Time to go and be a good sister for once."

"Sure," Eve replied, "but if you think of anything that might help, you'll let me know, won't you? Even if it seems insignificant, it could be important."

Charlotte nodded cautiously.

"I really think we'll find her," Eve continued. "I know the media's always full of terrible stories about young children who go missing, but those are just the cases that end badly. You wouldn't believe how many other kids disappear for a few hours and then turn up right as rain, and it never gets reported." She paused. "We're doing everything we can."

"I'm sure she'll turn up soon," Charlotte replied. "And, hell, if she doesn't, I guess she might come back in a year, right? Just like I did?"

Twenty years ago

Charlotte didn't know why, but she was starting to get short of breath. Beyond the pain and the fear, it was as if her chest was getting smaller and smaller, and she was taking in big gulps of air in an attempt to stop feeling as if she was suffocating.

Wedged between two rocks, she felt too weak to call out for help. At the same time, she was starting to worry that her mother wasn't going to come and find her at all. Summoning up the very last of her strength, she tried to ease herself up, ignoring the sensation of her snapped ankle dangling from the bottom of her leg, held on by little more than a section of skin and meat.

"Mummy," she whispered, hoping that maybe if screaming didn't help, something else might attract her mother's attention.

Slowly, she inched forward. She had no idea which way to go, but she figured her best bet was to keep going up. Reaching out, she tried to get some kind of grip on the cold, wet rocks. It was difficult, but eventually she felt confident enough to try pulling herself up. No matter how weak she felt and how much pain was coursing through her body, she knew she had no choice but to keep trying.

"Mummy?" she called out, before realizing that maybe someone else could help. "Ruth!" she shouted, hoping against hope that her older sister might hear. "Ruth! Help me!"

She continued with her desperate climb. No-one called back to answer her cries for help. The only sound in the cave, apart from her hands scrabbling at the rocks, was a distant dripping sound and the faintest hint of running water, along with an occasional howl of wind. For several minutes, Charlotte continued to haul herself up the side of a nearby rock, until finally she was on level ground. She stayed perfectly still for a moment, trying to ignore the crippling cold water that had soaked through her dress.

Deciding that she must be close to the exit of the cave by now, she dragged herself forward. She still felt breathless, but the sensation was no longer quite so bad and at least she didn't feel as if she was suffocating. She pulled herself across the rock, hoping that she might spot a hint of light up ahead, but there was nothing. She had no idea how far into the cave she'd fallen, but she kept telling herself that she'd be okay if she kept going up. All she had to do was -

Without warning, her right hand slipped on the rock, and in trying to steady herself, she turned and slipped, tumbling back down into the darkness. She slammed hard against another rock, bashing her broken ankle in the process, and then she rolled further down into the pitch black cave. Just as she was starting to wonder if she'd ever stop falling, she plunged headfirst into a freezing cold pool of water.

Today

By midnight, the area around the bottom of the garden and along the riverbank was crawling with police. Charlotte, Ruth and Tony took turns standing by the kitchen window, staring absently at the light display as men with torches searched the undergrowth and a solitary police helicopter circled above, casting its spotlight down toward the nearby fields. In the distance, there was the occasional bark of a police dog, and a little further away there were the multi-colored lights of a diving team, searching the river.

"What's the temperature out there?" Ruth asked, her face devoid of any emotion at all as she sat at the kitchen table while a long-since-boiled cup of tea cooled in front of her.

Tony looked over at the thermometer on the wall. "Five," he muttered after a moment.

"She wasn't wearing a jacket," Ruth said, her voice steady and flat, her reddened eyes staring down at the table. "She'll be cold. She..." Pausing, she took a deep breath. "If she's outside, she'll be so cold."

"She's probably holed up somewhere warm," Charlotte muttered, taking the pack of cigarettes out of her pocket and laying it on the table.

"You can't smoke in here," Ruth said suddenly.

"I'm not going to smoke in here," Charlotte snapped back at her.

Ruth's face twitched for a moment, as if she was struggling to hold back a blast of anger.

"Twenty-four hours," Tony said, staring out the window. "That's what they said earlier. The first twenty-four hours are crucial. There's a very good chance -"

"There's a very good chance she won't be back in twenty-four hours," Ruth replied, interrupting him. "And then what?"

"They're not going to stop looking," he pointed out.

"They spent weeks searching for me," Charlotte added.

Ruth turned to her.

"It's true," Charlotte continued. "Mum told me. They combed the entire area with fucking millimeter precision, looking for anything that might help."

"But they *didn't* find you, did they?" Ruth replied coldly. "You found yourself, a year later. Or at least that's what you've always told people."

"Not this again," Charlotte sighed. "You know, the -"

"Are you sure you don't remember what happened to you during that year?" Ruth continued, ignoring her sister's pained protests. "I mean, are you *really* sure? Because if something's holding you back, maybe vanity or embarrassment or shame, now's the time to put other people first and come clean, Charlotte. If you know anything that might explain what's happened to my daughter -"

"I don't!" Charlotte said, raising her voice a little before realizing that she needed to stay calm. "I don't remember anything."

"Because you're stubborn," Ruth snapped back at her.

"This isn't about me," Charlotte replied, grabbing a cigarette from the pack and heading to the back door. "This is about Sophie. She's going to be back soon. I can feel it in my gut." She was lying, but she figured it was better than admitting that she had a bad feeling about things. "Don't lose track of the fact that you need to focus on -"

"Don't tell me what to focus on," Ruth replied. "You're not a mother, Charlotte, and you never will be. You don't have a fucking clue what this is like." She paused. "You're nothing but a liar."

"What the hell have I lied about?" Charlotte asked.

"You remember where you were," Ruth continued. "Maybe other people believe your bullshit story about amnesia, but you remember. I can see it in your eyes."

Smiling sadly, Charlotte turned and headed out onto the porch, where she immediately lit the cigarette before stepping down onto the grass and starting to make her way across the lawn. She passed the deckchairs, which were still laid out from the afternoon, and eventually she made her way all the way down to the end of the garden, which overlooked the tow-path running alongside the river. All she wanted was to get away from the house, away from her sister's baseless accusations.

"Stop!" a voice shouted from the darkness.

Stopping in her tracks, Charlotte shielded her eyes as a torch swung toward her.

"I'm Charlotte Abernathy!" she called out after a moment. "I just came down to see if there's any news!"

The torch was lowered, and a dark figure stepped closer, eventually revealed to be the male officer from earlier.

"There's nothing you can do down here," he said calmly. "This is a potential crime scene, so I'm going to have to ask you to go up to the house and stay there while we continue our investigation."

"Crime scene?" Charlotte replied, shocked by the implication. "You're not -"

"We're covering all bases," the officer said firmly. "I'm sure you'll understand that we can't rule anything out at this stage. We should have a better idea of what we're dealing with in the morning, so if you'll please return to the house, I need to get back to work. We've decided to extend the operation through the night, in recognition of the urgency of the case, so we'll be here for the foreseeable future, at least until we find Sophie."

"Sure," Charlotte muttered, taking a drag on her cigarette before turning and starting the walk back toward the house. After a few paces, she glanced over her shoulder and saw that the torch was still aimed straight at her, as if the police officer was watching her leave. She knew she was probably just being a little paranoid, but Charlotte couldn't stop worrying that in some way, her past made her a natural target for suspicion. As she reached the back door, she turned and looked out at the darkened countryside. The thought of Sophie being out there, lost and alone or maybe even worse, was too much to deal with, but she'd never been the kind of person to let her emotions get on top of her. All she could do was hope that wherever she was, Sophie was okay.

She had to be.

Twenty years ago

In the dream, or vision, or whatever it was...

She was sinking through ice-cold water, her arms outstretched as if she was flying through the frozen darkness, her eyes wide open. Although she was aware on one level that she was in danger, on another level she thought nothing of it. Her eyes were closed and everything was beautiful.

It was as if she didn't need to breathe at all. Not ever again, not even as she bumped against the muddy bottom of the pool.

Today

Sleep was impossible that night, so after a while Charlotte didn't even try.

    Balancing on a small footstool, she stood in the middle of the guest bedroom and carefully unscrewed the smoke detector from the ceiling. It was a delicate job, and she was more than a little worried that her sister might have booby-trapped the device in anticipation of such a move. Many had been the argument, over the years, about Charlotte's inability (or unwillingness, according to Ruth) to quit "that filthy habit", but such concerns didn't seem to matter so much on that long, terrified night following Sophie's disappearance. Finally - with the dexterity and calm concentration of Indiana Jones in some far-off temple - Charlotte was able to slip the detector out of its mounting and slide the back open to reveal the battery. She paused for a moment, before pulling the slip of fabric that brought the battery out of its slot, and the evil flashing red light was defeated.

    Two minutes later, Charlotte was sitting by the open window, smoking the best cigarette of her life. She knew smoking was bad for her, of course, but then so were lots of other things: crossing the road, eating junk food, coloring her hair, living in London, staying up late at night browsing the internet, having sex with strangers, not having sex with anyone, drinking alone... She'd once tried to cut out all the damaging behavior in her life, and the result had been utter tedium. Some people went through life on rails, but Charlotte simply couldn't help barreling along, collecting cuts and dents along the way; she was the kind of person who just figured she'd be okay, that her body would accept a little rough and tumble, and that consequences were things that happened to other people.

Beyond the window, and beyond the lawn, and perhaps even beyond life itself, there were still lights down by the river. Police divers, Charlotte figured, were out there in the cold water, searching for something macabre and horrific: the dead body of a young girl, just eight years old, who might have tumbled beneath the surface and been unable to keep herself from sinking. For a fraction of a second, she imagined Sophie's body down there, picked out by the granular searchlights of the diving team, her dead eyes reflecting the sad but hardened faces of the divers as they realized their search was over. Charlotte kept telling herself that Sophie would be okay, of course; like a good aunt, like a good person, she repeated that phrase over and over in her head like a mantra.

Still, in the back of her mind, there was a voice...

She took a long, deep puff on her cigarette and tried to make her thoughts fall silent for a moment. Unfortunately, when the thoughts went away, their place was taken by gruesome images of a dead Sophie. Blinking a couple of times, Charlotte decided to embrace the thoughts instead of the images.

Hearing a noise below the window, she leaned out and saw a figure shuffling out of the back door. She frowned for a moment as she recognized the unmistakeable gait of her mother, who seemed to have decided to take a post-midnight stroll. For a couple of seconds, Charlotte tried to work out what the old bat was doing outside at almost two in the morning, but finally she got to her feet and headed out of the guest room. She knew she should stub the cigarette out, and that her sister would undoubtedly be able to trace its lingering scent in the morning, but at this particular moment Charlotte didn't give a damn. When she got down into the hallway, she held the cigarette between her teeth as she put her coat on over the thin t-shirt she'd worn to bed, and then she headed out the front door into the ice-cold night.

"What are you doing out here?" she whispered as she came up behind her mother, her breath visible in the cold night air. "It's fucking freezing!"

Looking shocked that she'd been spotted, the old woman turned to her daughter.

"You been sleep-walking or something?" Charlotte asked.

Slowly, her mother shook her head.

"Just thought you'd come out and freeze to death, did you?" As soon as she'd said the words, Charlotte regretted being so harsh. She usually enjoyed finding inventive ways to harangue her mother, but tonight seemed different. "It's kinda nippy, don't you think?"

"I just..."

There was an awkward silence, and the old woman seemed a little confused.

"Come inside," Charlotte continued, taking her by the arm. "I'll pour you a sherry." She waited for a reply, and for the first time in many years, she actually felt a little sorry for her mother. She knew the feeling wouldn't last, of course, but she also knew there was no point fighting it for now.

"Is she really missing?" her mother asked suddenly, resisting the attempt to lead her back inside and, instead, staring at the lights down by the river. "I thought maybe it had been a bad dream."

"Sure," Charlotte replied. "Everything's been a bad dream, ever since I was born. Go back to sleep, and when you wake up in the morning, it'll be the mid-eighties again. Whoop-de-doo."

"Sophie's missing," her mother replied. "That's right, isn't it?"

"I'm sure they'll find her soon," Charlotte replied wearily. "Come on, Mum. We need to get you back inside before you drop dead of pneumonia."

The old woman still resisted, as if the lights of the police search crews were mesmerizing her. "Or is it Charlotte?" she asked after a moment. "I don't remember. Which of them is out there?"

Charlotte paused. This wasn't the first time she'd suspected her mother of losing her marbles, and she doubted it'd be the last. Whether it was Parkinson's or Alzheimer's or just old age, something was riddling the old woman's mind.

"Mum," Charlotte continued, "please, don't make me leave you out here. I will, you know. I'm that much of a bitch." She took a puff on her cigarette, and the warmth felt good in her chest. "Mum, please," she added, desperate to get back into the relative warmth of the darkened kitchen.

"It was like this when Charlotte went missing, you know," her mother replied, as if she hadn't heard her. "Lights, just like this. They were in the water, trying to find her. They said they thought she'd be okay, but they still looked in all the places where a dead child might be found. I could see it in their eyes, you know. Before they even walked in the door, they thought she was gone." She paused, and a look of utter confusion crossed her face. "It's Sophie, isn't it? It's Sophie who's missing now?"

Charlotte nodded.

"She's Ruth's child. Not Charlotte's. Charlotte doesn't have any children. I think she may be barren."

"Thanks a lot," Charlotte muttered.

"It's like a replay," her mother said. "It's like..." Her voice trailed off, and she seemed utterly lost in her thoughts. "Poor Charlotte. I hope they find her eventually."

"It's Sophie," Charlotte replied, a little spooked by her mother's words. "Sophie's the one who's missing. *I'm* Charlotte, remember? I'm right here, see?"

Her mother stared at her for a moment, as if her thoughts were slowly congealing.

"I'm freezing my tits off," Charlotte continued, taking another puff on her cigarette. "Can we *please* just get inside? I'll stay up and talk to you, whatever the fuck you want, but for God's sake, can we get out of the cold?"

"You go," her mother replied. "I'll be okay out here."

"Fine," Charlotte said, letting go of her mother's arm and turning back toward the door, before suddenly realizing that no matter how much she hated the old woman, and no matter how cold she was, something was preventing her from leaving her outside alone. It wasn't affection or pity, and she was damn sure it wasn't love or human compassion, but for some damn reason, she sighed and turned back to her mother. "You're lucky I'm so kind," she said after a moment. "You are so damn fucking lucky that I'm a decent fucking human being."

"It's my fault," her mother replied quietly, all the fight and confidence gone from her voice. "That poor girl. Such a horrible way to die."

"She's not dead," Charlotte replied wearily. "Please don't say things like that, especially not around Ruth. You'll do her head in, Mum."

"It's so sad, and it's all my fault."

"It's really not," Charlotte told her, before pausing for a moment. "Wait, do you mean this thing with Sophie, or the broader dysfunctional mess of the family? 'Cause if you mean the thing with Sophie, then it's really not your fault at all. The other thing? Maybe there are a few issues..." She waited for a reply, before finally realizing that she needed to do or say something to catch her mother's attention and break her out of this reverie. "I meant what I said," she continued eventually, surprising herself. "What happened to me, it wasn't your fault."

"What are you talking about?" her mother asked, turning to her with a sharp, shocked look in her eyes. "Nothing happened to you."

"You're really not okay, are you?" Charlotte asked with a heavy heart. "Jesus, you're out of it."

"I hope they find her body soon."

"For Sophie's sake -"

"Why would it help Sophie?" her mother replied, seemingly annoyed. "What good would rummaging around in anyone's head do for that poor little girl, eh? Sophie's... Sophie's a lovely child. Warm and happy and playful, not like that poor little..." Her voice trailed off, and for a moment she looked utterly horrified.

"Sophie could still be okay," Charlotte said eventually.

"This isn't about you, Charlotte," her mother said, suddenly seeming much more energized as she shuffled back past her and into the kitchen. "Everything that happened to you is in the past, and Sophie is very much in the present. It's Sophie who must be the focus of our attention, and there's no point going rooting around in events that were put to bed a long time ago. The past is the past, and the present is the present. Please, child, for the sake of all that's holy in the world, don't go talking nonsense."

Sighing, Charlotte followed her inside and pushed the door shut. "Sorry," she muttered, figuring that at least the old woman seemed to have drifted into a moment of lucidity. "Didn't mean to put a jolt up your ass."

"This isn't a game," her mother continued, making her way slowly toward the hallway. "It's not a puzzle. It's just a coincidence, that's all. Whatever has happened to that poor, sweet little girl, it's nothing to do with what happened to you. Please, dear, don't muddy the waters." She paused, before turning back to Charlotte. "You don't understand. You never did, and you never will."

Charlotte opened her mouth to reply, but something made her hold back. The transformation in her mother was surprising: in just a couple of seconds, the old woman had gone from seeming sad, confused and melancholy to seeming angry and defensive, and Charlotte couldn't help but feel that she'd accidentally touched a nerve. She felt bad for thinking such a thing, but she actually preferred her mother when the dementia was in full force.

"Do you want a glass of sherry?" she asked, hoping to calm the waters.

No reply.

"Mum?"

Without saying anything, her mother turned and started to make her way upstairs.

"Don't offer to help," she called back. "I can manage. I'd hate for you to break a sweat and help an old lady up the stairs."

"Cool," Charlotte replied.

She stood in silence for a few minutes, listening to her mother's pained journey up to her room. Sighing, she took another puff on her cigarette and tried to decide whether or not to down the entire bottle of sherry herself. She wasn't tired, and she knew the following day was going to be exhausting and draining. Walking over to the sink, she looked out the window and watched as the now-familiar lights continued to blaze down by the river, signaling the continued work of the police as they searched for Sophie. All that comforting talk of the first twenty-four hours was now starting to seem somewhat doom-laden, and when she tried to think of reasons why Sophie would have gone away and stayed out all night, she came up with nothing comforting. Taking another puff on the cigarette, she tried to imagine the little girl out there somewhere, still alive but cold and frightened, maybe hurt, maybe in danger, maybe crying.

"Please," she whispered eventually, hoping that someone - maybe God, maybe someone else - might be able to hear her. "Please, let Sophie be alright. Bring her home. I don't care what else you take, but bring Sophie home to -"

Before she could finish, an ear-piercing alarm began to scream almost directly above her head, shattering the quiet of the night and causing Charlotte to drop her cigarette into the sink as she clamped her hands over her ears. Looking up, she saw the tell-tale flashing red light of a smoke detector in the middle of the kitchen ceiling, and seconds later she heard the sound of her sister and brother-in-law bounding from their beds and hurrying down to see what was wrong.

"Balls," Charlotte muttered bitterly.

Twenty years ago

When she woke up, Charlotte was wet and cold and still in darkness, but she was alive and - to her surprise - she realized she was no longer underwater.

Sitting up, she found that there was still a small amount of water around her waist, but it seemed as if most of the ice cold liquid had somehow drained away. She sat in silence for a moment, taking slow, steady breaths as she tried to work out what the hell was happening to her. The pain in her ankle had reduced to a dull throb, but she figured that any reduction in pain was probably because the freezing water had numbed most of her body. She reached around and found several rocks nearby, and finally she decided that she had to try to find a way out.

"Mummy!" she shouted, hauling herself up onto one leg, while carefully trying to keep her other, damaged leg from touching anything. "Ruth! Help!"

She waited, but the only reply was a faint echo of her own voice.

"Ettolrahc," she whispered. "Please, I need you."

After a moment, she realized that she was starting to shiver. Reaching up, she felt ice crystals in her hair. She'd already fallen twice now, each time tumbling down into the darkness, and she was sure she must be a long way underground by now. She opened her mouth to shout for help, but finally it occurred to her that no-one could hear her, even if they were looking. Figuring that she should probably conserve energy, she decided to focus on finding her own way out of the cave. After all, it was clear that for whatever reason, no-one was coming to save her. Not her mother. Not Ruth. Not Ettolrahc. No-one.

Today

"Who puts a smoke alarm in the kitchen?" Charlotte asked as she used a spoon to take an egg out of the boiling water and slip it into an eggcup. She wasn't usually the kind of person who embraced smalltalk, but right now she was desperate to fill the silence with words, any words, even if they were utterly pointless. "I mean, really, that's just asking for trouble. Don't you ever burn dinner? Don't you constantly set the damn thing off every time you get stuff out from the microwave?"

Turning, she saw that Ruth was sitting at the kitchen table with her head in her hands, patently uninterested in anything that her sister was saying.

"So I had *one* cigarette," Charlotte continued, standing by the kitchen counter while she waited for her toast to pop up. "It's not a crime. I know you don't *like* them in the house, and I'm sorry, but I didn't mean to wake everyone up. It's not like I burned the house down or anything. I'm careful, and I always do it by a window, so there's no smell." She waited for her sister to say something, anything, but instead the silent gulf between them seemed to be widening with every second. "They're pretty good for stress," she added. "If you want to try one, just let me know."

Ruth turned and scowled at her.

"I'm sorry," Charlotte added. "I just -"

"Do you think," Ruth said suddenly, her voice firm with anger as she picked her words carefully, "for one fucking moment, that I give a crap about your fucking cigarettes?" Her eyes red and puffy from crying all night, she looked as if she was just about ready to kill someone. "Seriously?" she continued. "Do you think I give a damn what you do? Do you think it's a matter of concern to me at this precise moment in time?" She paused, as if she was trying to think of some fresh way to voice her disapproval. "You can smoke yourself to death right in front of me for all I care. If you smoking and killing yourself with fucking lung cancer would bring my daughter back right now, I would *gladly* take that deal in a heartbeat."

The toast popped up.

"It's true," Ruth continued. "I would. I *really* would."

"You know what I mean," Charlotte said, turning away from her sister and trying not to get too freaked out by the unprecedented venom in her words. She and Ruth had always had a somewhat adversarial, sparring repartee, but this was something new. For the first time, Charlotte felt that she was actually loathed and despised, and her hands were trembling as she grabbed a knife from the drawer. It was as if, suddenly, all her weapons had been blunted. "I'm just sorry for waking you up," she said quietly as she buttered her burned toast. "That's all."

"I wasn't asleep," Ruth said wearily. "What kind of mother could sleep at a time like this?"

"Sorry."

"I spent the whole night trying to call out to her," Ruth continued. "Not literally. I mean, with my mind. I kept hoping that somehow I could sense where she was, that maybe..." She paused. "I know it sounds stupid, but I felt it was worth a try. I thought that maybe we could hear each other, across the distance. All I needed was silence, so I could concentrate. We've always been so close, and I just hoped that maybe there might be some way for us to communicate." She sighed. "It was a stupid idea."

"Sorry."

"Stop apologizing," she shot back. "It makes me feel physically sick."

Keeping her mouth shut, Charlotte looked down at her meager breakfast and realized she wasn't remotely hungry. She knew she should eat something, but she was convinced that even a mouthful of food would make her vomit. She couldn't help feeling that, no matter how bad things were, they were poised to get inexorably worse at any moment. A knock on the door, a phone call, an e-mail... there were so many ways that bad news could arrive, and she almost felt as if they were under siege.

"How's Tony this morning?" she asked eventually.

"How do you think?"

"I guess he didn't sleep either, huh?"

"Is this all you've got to offer?" Ruth asked. "Asinine questions? You can't help, you can't do anything constructive, so you just stand around uttering these fucking ridiculous platitudes? Jesus Christ, Charlotte, did anyone ever tell you that you're fucking hopeless in a crisis? I mean, really, Jesus, you're completely useless."

"So you're swearing again, huh?" Charlotte replied with a faint smile.

"My daughter's not here, is she?" Ruth shouted, losing control for a moment before regathering her composure. "If you've got nothing useful to say," she continued eventually, "then it might be better to keep quiet. There's no point filling the silence with inane chatter. I need to think."

"I helped Mum last night," Charlotte said defensively. "She was wandering out the door at two in the morning wearing nothing but her nightgown, and I steered her back inside."

"Great," Ruth muttered. "I'll arrange for you to receive a medal, shall I? After all, I took the old bitch in, I gave her a home, I feed her and wash her clothes and keep her stocked with sherry, I listen to her inane drivel all day every day, but you're the daughter of the fucking year because you dragged her saggy ass back into the fucking house one night.

You're clearly as good a daughter as you are a sister. You must be so fucking proud of yourself."

Charlotte stared at her sister for a moment, unsure as to what to say. All the jokes and sarcasm of the past few days seemed wildly inappropriate. She couldn't shake the feeling that all the bile and anger spilling out of Ruth had been bubbling away for years, and had been waiting for a time like this so that it could be heard. She knew that her sister was hurting, but she also knew that even if Sophie ran through the door at that exact moment, things would never be the same again. She wanted to leave, but she knew she had to stay. For now, at least. She couldn't run out on Ruth now, even if she hated her.

Still sitting at the kitchen table, Ruth sighed as she put her head in her hands.

"Sophie's going to be okay," Charlotte offered eventually, even though she knew her words sounded hollow. "I can just feel it, Ruth. She's going to come back through the door soon, and you're all going to be together again, and it's going to turn out that this has all been some kind of huge misunderstanding, and she'll be right back here with you -"

"In a *year*, like you?" Ruth snapped. "Is that what's going to happen? Is my daughter going to vanish and spend a year in whatever mystical shitty far-off land you went to, and then she'll come back and have no memory of what happened to her, but it'll all be okay because she'll be fine, is that what's going to happen?" She paused. "Is my daughter going to end up like *you*?"

"There are worse things," Charlotte replied with a faint, tentative smile.

"Not many," Ruth said firmly. "She'd probably be better off dead. I mean, look at you, Charlotte. You're... empty."

Charlotte looked down at her breakfast again. She knew that anything she said right now would just be taken the wrong way, but at the same time, she wanted to help her sister.

"You never really came back, you know," Ruth continued after a moment. "You walked through the door all those years ago, but you were different. It was like a ghost of you came back, but the rest of you stayed away. I knew it from the moment I first saw you again. Everyone else was fussing around and saying how wonderful it was that you'd come home after a year, and I couldn't work out why they didn't see the difference. Something was missing from you, and it still is, and that's why you're cracked down the middle. You just never really came back."

Charlotte took a deep breath. Everything her sister was saying was true, but it still hurt to hear the words.

"Do you want to know something else?" Ruth continued. "I think you know *exactly* what happened to you while you were missing. I think all this bullshit about not remembering is a cover story. You just don't want to tell anyone. That's why you've never agreed to go and get therapy, because you know your bullshit wouldn't work the same way. A psychiatrist would see through your lies and force you to tell the truth, and that's the last thing you want, so you put up this facade of toughness as an excuse."

They stood in silence for a moment.

"I think I should go up and get changed," Charlotte said eventually, feeling as if she needed to get the hell away from her sister for a few minutes before she ended up telling her to go fuck herself. "I'm going to go down to the river and see if I can help, so -"

"You can help by telling us all what really happened to you," Ruth said firmly. "Anything else is just noise."

Without replying, Charlotte turned and hurried out of the kitchen, leaving her breakfast uneaten. By the time she got up to the guest room, there were tears in her eyes, and soon she was sitting on the bed with her back to the wall and her knees drawn up to her chin, trying desperately to hold herself together. She kept hearing her sister's words cutting through her mind, and she knew full well that, in Ruth's eyes at least, it was her fault that Sophie was missing. Still, no matter how hard she tried, she couldn't remember what had happened to her all those years ago. She knew that even if she *did* go and get help, and even if that help *did* unlock her memories, there was no way that it'd help in the search for Sophie; all that would happen would be that Ruth would move on and find some other reason to attack her.

With tears flowing down her cheeks, she started to sob uncontrollably. The worst part was that, almost her entire life, she'd felt that there was a locked, impassable door in her mind, hiding all the secrets away; for the first time, however, she was started to feel as if a small, childish hand was pawing at that door, slowly teasing it open and threatening to reveal the truth. Charlotte had never understood why other people felt that the truth was so important. To her, a good lie could paper over a thousand ugly truths, and she didn't see a damn thing wrong with that arrangement.

Twenty years ago

With two undamaged ankles, climbing up the rock-face would have been difficult; with one good ankle and one that was broken, the job was almost impossible.

Still, she couldn't give up.

"Look," she whispered, with tears in her eyes, "I'm trying. I'm not scared." The pain in her belly was getting worse, however, as if Ettolrahc was still dead. "Come back."

Each new grip had to be judged carefully. She'd been climbing for a few minutes now, but she knew that one wrong move would undo all her work and send her tumbling back down into the depths. Her arms were aching and she was feeling light-headed, but she was certain that she'd die if she stopped to rest. Since there was no light, she couldn't see her broken ankle, but she figured she'd probably lost a lot of blood.

The worst part, though, was that she was alone. Her other half, her adventurous and brave half, was nowhere to be found. It was as if only her meek half had fallen, and her adventurous half had stayed up at the mouth of the cave, laughing at her misfortune. Suddenly it occurred to Charlotte that maybe her entire body had split in two, and the reason no-one had come to look for her was that she had a doppelganger who had gone back to the house. Perhaps, she wondered, she had been left down in the cave to die by a stronger version of herself who just wanted to get rid of her. Then again, maybe there was a simpler explanation: maybe her family were glad that she'd vanished, and they were hoping she'd stay away. She took a deep breath as she tried to tell herself that she was imagining things, but deep down, she felt there had to be some kind of explanation. Why had no-one arrived at the cave to look for her?

"Please let me get out of here," she whispered, hoping that God might take pity on her. Hauling herself up onto another rock, she paused for a moment to get her breath back. "Please," she continued eventually, "help me get home. I don't want to be down here. I'm cold. I'll be good, I swear. I'll never, ever do anything bad ever again, and I won't think anything mean, and I'll spend my whole life doing good things for other people if you just let me get out of here."

All around her, there was nothing but silence and darkness. She waited for some kind of sign that someone, anyone, might be listening to her prayers, but finally tears began to roll down her cheeks as she realized that no-one was coming to help her. She turned, figuring she should continue her climb, but in her panic she let her foot slip and she began to tumble back down. At the last moment, she was able to grab a section of rock and hold on tight, with her legs and body dangling down into the darkness. Reaching up, she tried to haul herself back to the top of a nearby rock.

Today

"I'd go crazy," said Eve Locklear as she and Charlotte walked along the riverbank. "A whole year, missing from my memory, would drive me completely round the bend. I just couldn't function."

Charlotte opened her mouth to reply, but at the last moment she realized that she wasn't quite sure what to say. Pretty much every person she'd met over the years had said the same thing: that a gap in their mind would be intolerable, and that they'd have to seek help in order to fill that gap in and find out the truth. Charlotte had come to realize that her own reaction - which amounted to little more than mild curiosity - was abnormal, and she couldn't help but wonder *why* she was so calm and rational about the whole thing. When she was younger, she'd considered herself to be lucky, and she'd ascribed her reaction to strength and good character; lately, however, she was starting to wonder if there wasn't something deeply wrong with her. What kind of trauma, she wondered, could cause someone to not only forget their ordeal, but could even cause them to not be curious?

"So how do you do it?" Eve continued, with a faint smile. "How do you manage to keep from going nuts?"

"Who says I manage?" Charlotte replied.

"You're walking around," Eve pointed out, "and you seem to hold down a job. Most people in your position would be jabbering away in the corner of a padded cell."

"It's hard to be too badly affected by something I don't remember," Charlotte replied. "I suppose I could go to therapy or try to force a few memories up from the depths of my mind, but what would be the point? Just so I could go nicely wacky?"

"That's a very rational way of looking at it. I doubt many people would be able to see things the same way."

"Here," Charlotte said suddenly, stopping about twenty meters from the cave. She turned to look back the way they'd come, and she tried to ignore the police boat slowly making its way along the river as its crew continued their grim search. "Right here."

"So the first thing you remember after your missing year," Eve replied, "is standing in this spot?"

"Not standing," Charlotte replied. "Walking. The very beginning of my memory is..." She looked down at the muddy ground. "I was just walking along here, making my way back to the house."

"So that would be..." Eve paused as she checked her bearings. "You were walking away from the cave?"

Charlotte nodded.

"And at that time," Eve continued, "did you have any idea that you'd been missing for so long? I mean, what were you thinking?"

"I'm not sure I was thinking about anything, really," Charlotte admitted. "My mother said later that I was in a kind of daze when I arrived back at the house. She said I was a little dirty, and I was limping, and my clothes were torn, but otherwise I was pretty much okay." She paused. "Quiet. She said I was very quiet."

"You were wearing the same clothes you'd been wearing when you disappeared?"

Charlotte nodded again. "My mother immediately got them off me and threw them out. She burned them, actually."

"And I guess you had a load of tests performed," Eve replied. "Physical and mental?"

"No-one touched me," Charlotte replied. "That's what the reports said, and I have no reason not to believe them. I went completely unmolested."

"I looked up your case file last night," Eve continued, with a hint of awkwardness in her voice. "There's not really very much in there. From what I can tell, you just disappeared without a trace one day, and there was no sign of you at all until you wandered back to your mother's house. Every effort was made to find you while you were missing, and then to work out where you'd been once you came back, but nothing helped." She paused. "What about your father? If you don't mind the question..."

"Dead," Charlotte replied. "I don't even remember him, but he died just after I was born. I've seen photos. He sounds like a nice man. If you want my opinion..." She paused as she realized that maybe she should hold back.

"What?" Eve asked.

"I was just going to say that the wrong parent died," Charlotte continued. "God, I sound like a total bitch, don't I? The truth is, my mother and I have never really managed to get along. She's always seemed so nervous around me, almost like she's scared of me."

"Was she like that before you disappeared?" Eve asked.

"I have no idea," Charlotte replied. "My memories of life before that year are..." She tried to think of the right word. "Sketchy," she added eventually. "I remember flashes, images, things like that, but nothing concrete. I guess my year away must have really fucked with my head, huh?" She paused for a moment, before turning to Eve. "She's losing her mind now. Some kind of dementia, although no-one's had it checked out. She gets everything mixed up. Last night, she was acting as if it was twenty years ago and I was the one who was missing."

"She seemed a little confused when I spoke to her," Eve replied.

"A *little* confused?" Charlotte smiled. "Sounds like you caught her on a good day." She paused. "So the worst-case scenario here is... what? That Sophie stays missing for a year, and then maybe, just maybe, she turns up, the way I did?"

"The odds of that are very slim," Eve pointed out. "We can't count on miracles here."

"But that's what it was," Charlotte continued. "A miracle. When I turned up." She looked down at her hands. "Sometimes I feel as if I didn't come back at all."

"Then how am I talking to you?" Eve replied with a smile.

"Maybe *you're* nuts," Charlotte muttered, turning and looking down into the water. Once again, she was finding it hard to banish horrific images from her mind: images of Sophie's dead body bumping lifelessly along the riverbed, eventually being found at the estuary with her eyes being pecked out by seagulls.

"Divers have searched the river for several miles," Eve explained. "Based on our best estimates, she couldn't have been washed more than five miles away. We're in the middle of a second check of a ten mile stretch, just to be absolutely certain, but it's looking increasingly unlikely that Sophie went into the water. Besides, it's not as if the river's particularly deep along this stretch, and the current's not strong."

Charlotte continued to stare at the river for a moment. "Then where the hell is she?" she asked eventually.

They stood in silence for a few seconds.

"Maybe she's in the same place that you were for a year," Eve said eventually.

Charlotte turned to her.

"It's the only lead we have at the moment," Eve continued. "You said you've never made much of an attempt to dig into your past, but... Even though it might not be something you want to do right now, would you consider seeing someone? Odds are, it won't help at all, but if there's even a chance that it might help Sophie..." She left the end of the sentence hanging, hoping to encourage Charlotte to finish the thought for her. "When two unexplained things happen in the same way in the same place to the same family," she added eventually, "we'd be fools not to take a look at the possibilities."

"It'd be a needless distraction," Charlotte replied cautiously. She was used to fending off such requests from her sister, but it was harder to argue with Eve.

"Probably," Eve replied, "but if there's even a chance that it might help, then surely it's worth considering the possibility? If not for your sake, then maybe for Sophie's?"

Although she was tempted to agree, Charlotte couldn't help but think back to her mother's words the previous night. All her life, her mother had been the sole voice supporting her decision not to seek therapy, and she was tempted to defy the old woman purely out of spite. Then again, she was also scared of what she might discover, and she was certain there could be no link between the events that had conspired to spirit Sophie away, and the events that had taken place twenty years earlier.

"Maybe she was abducted," Charlotte said after a moment, giving voice to the fear that she'd been nurturing since the previous night. "If she didn't have an accident, then someone must have chosen to take her away. Someone who..." She paused, not wanting to consider the full implications of this possibility. "There are freaks in the world," she continued after a few seconds. "I mean, you're a cop, right? I don't need to tell you that there are some fucking evil bastards out there."

"I'm well aware of that," Eve replied calmly.

"Sophie was a quiet, shy girl," Charlotte continued, before realizing that she'd begun to think of her niece in the past tense. "I mean, she *is* a quiet, shy girl," she added, "and although she's been taught not to talk to strangers, it's still possible that someone might have... lured her..." Her voice trailed off as she realized she was on the verge of tears. Glancing over her shoulder for a moment, she looked along the towpath. "We didn't hear any vehicles yesterday afternoon," she added after a moment, hoping that the emotion wasn't evident in her voice, "but that doesn't mean that someone couldn't have been here. Watching us. Waiting for an opportunity."

"That's a possibility that we're looking into with active interest," Eve replied. "We're checking to see if any known offenders might have been in the area, and we're looking at camera footage from various locations in the area to see if anything suspicious is apparent."

"Like what?" Charlotte asked, turning back to her. "A car driving past with a pair of girl's legs sticking out the fucking boot?" She paused. "Sorry, that was totally unnecessary."

Eve smiled patiently. "Nothing so dramatic, fortunately," she continued, evidently trying to calm Charlotte's fears. "We're following multiple avenues of investigation simultaneously until we can narrow the search down."

"And how long are you going to give it?" Charlotte asked. "Before you give up and decide that she must be dead?"

"That's not a -"

"Five weeks," Charlotte added, interrupting her. There were tears in her eyes now, but she knew there was no point trying to hide them. "That's how long they looked for me when I disappeared twenty years ago. Five fucking weeks, and then they packed up and said they've just have to continue the investigation in a more stripped-down form back at the station. They basically assumed I was dead and gave up."

"We *never* give up -"

"Yes," Charlotte continued, finally giving voice to the anger that had been simmering since the previous night. "At some point, people are going to give up and accept that Sophie's dead, just like they gave up and accepted that *I* was dead. It's just human nature, and..." She paused as she finally realized she was becoming too emotional. "No-one found me twenty years ago," she added. "Wherever I was, I got out of there myself, and I made my own way home, and when I got to the back door, everyone assumed I was a fucking ghost. Sometimes, it's as if they *still* think I'm a ghost, like I never really came back. And do you know something else? They're right. That's exactly how it feels!"

"We're going to find Sophie," Eve said, her voice filled with doubt. "I feel it in my -"

"Forget it," Charlotte said, turning and walking away. She sniffed back tears and wiped her eyes, determined to find somewhere she could be alone. She felt like a fool for having even considered getting therapy to deal with her amnesia. All she wanted, at that particular moment, was to hide away from the world and to never, ever have to see anyone again.

Twenty years ago

Sitting up with a jolt, Charlotte realized she must have passed out for a moment. She reached around frantically, terrified that she might have slipped further into the darkness, but finally she figured that it didn't really matter anyway.

She leaned back against the rock-face. Before she passed out, she was feeling weak; now, it was as if all the energy in her body had drained away. She tried to keep her eyes open, but from time to time they seemed to close automatically, as if they had a will of their own. After a while, she began to lose track of how much time passed between each moment of thought; she was fairly sure that every time she closed her eyes, minutes or hours were lost. She barely had the energy to think anymore, and she certainly couldn't shout for help.

So she waited. All around her, the cave walls were continuing to drip, and occasionally a splash of cold water landed on her skin. At first she flinched when she felt each drop, but gradually she lost the will for even that small act of life. She let her head droop down, her chin pressing against her chest, and something else began to change: whereas before she'd been mostly awake, now she was only occasionally opening her eyes, each time just for a few seconds before drowsiness carried her away again.

Slowly but surely, the gaps between consciousness were getting longer and longer, until finally she stopped waking up entirely and sank, instead, into permanent darkness.

Today

"It's Charlotte Abernathy," she said quietly as she leaned out the guest room door and double-checked that no-one was nearby, before pushing the door shut and walking over to the window. "I'd like to speak to Dr. Gould, please."

"Do you have a scheduled phone consultation today?" the receptionist asked with effortless, clinical professionalism, as if she'd dealt with a thousand such requests already that day.

"No, I just need to talk to him!"

"Dr. Gould requires patients to book phone consultations in advance," the receptionist continued with a steady, disinterested tone. "I could fit you in on Tuesday the eleventh at -"

"Now!" Charlotte hissed, careful to keep her voice down. "I need to speak to him right now! Tell him it's literally a matter of life and death."

"I can fit you in on Tuesday the eleventh," the receptionist replied calmly. "Dr. Gould has a very strict policy of not -"

"Tell him it's Charlotte Abernathy."

"His policy is -"

"Tell him it's Charlotte Abernathy and the police are involved."

"One moment," the receptionist replied, clearly sounding annoyed as she put Charlotte on hold.

Taking a deep breath, Charlotte looked out the window. There were a couple of police cars parked down near the river, but that didn't mean anything. Police had been swarming all over the place since the previous day, and now, just to add to the charm of the whole situation, a bunch of journalists had begun to sniff around, keen to get another 'missing child' story off the ground. They'd clearly twigged that Sophie was a telegenic young girl whose plight would attract the interest of the nation and, crucially, secure big ratings for the news channels.

Sighing, she considered putting the phone down. She'd been seeing Dr. Gould for a few years, although their therapy sessions were carefully designed to avoid directly prodding the mystery of her disappearance; instead, they always talked about her *current* life and problems. She'd never mentioned the sessions to her sister, preferring to keep these disparate parts of her life separate from one another, but finally she was starting to feel as if everything was coming crashing together.

"Hello, Charlotte," Dr. Gould said suddenly, his voice sounding calm and authoritative. "I'm sorry, I can't talk today, but -"

"My niece has gone missing," Charlotte hissed.

There was a pause on the other end of the line. "I'm sorry, can you -"

"My niece," she continued. "My sister's daughter, Sophie. She vanished yesterday, down by the river, right where I was when..." She paused for a moment. "You must have seen it on the news," she added. "Her name's Sophie. There have been police all over the place since yesterday afternoon. They've been looking everywhere, but..." She paused again, and finally she realized she was on the verge of tears again. "They're blaming me," she continued eventually. "I can tell. They think it's something to do with me."

"Who thinks that?" Dr. Gould asked, his voice locking into a calm, professional tone that made it clear he was willing to engage on the subject.

"Everyone," Charlotte replied. "I can tell by the way they're talking to me." She took a deep breath. "My niece hasn't been seen since yesterday lunchtime. She's eight years old and she just vanished down by the river."

There was another pause. "I see," Dr. Gould said uncomfortably.

"I don't know what to do," Charlotte continued, trying to slow her voice down and keep all her thoughts from tumbling out at once. "Everyone's looking at me like this is my fault!"

"I'm sure no-one's -"

"They are!" Charlotte hissed. "I can see it in their eyes, hear it in their voices... My sister's pretty much come out and said it, and the others... Even the police think it must be something to do with everything that happened to me. It's like they think I'm some kind of twisted bitch who brings devastation and disaster trailing in her wake wherever she goes. It's a cold day in hell when my mother turns out to be the most agreeable out of all of them, but that seems to be how it's going." She paused. "They blame me," she added eventually. "They just... do."

"I'm sure that's not possible," Dr. Gould replied. "Charlotte, I think there's a danger that you might be becoming paranoid -"

"I'm not paranoid!" she replied, raising her voice before remembering the need to keep quiet. "People are blaming me for not remembering what happened twenty years ago. They think I can help them work out what happened to Sophie, but I can't, can I? There's no way..." She took a deep breath as she tried to get her thoughts straight. "I feel like I'm losing my mind," she said eventually. "I keep telling myself that Sophie's disappearance can't be my fault, but it's as if somehow I'm missing something important. It can't be a coincidence, can it? It's just not possible..."

"It sounds highly unlikely," Dr. Gould replied, "but that doesn't mean it's your fault, Charlotte." He paused. "When are you coming back to London? I'd like to see you, and I think we should reconsider your earlier decision to -"

"No," Charlotte said firmly. "I'm not doing it."

"If -"

"No!"

Dr. Gould sighed. "I want you to listen to me very carefully, Charlotte," he continued after a moment. "Your niece's disappearance is not your fault. Even if there are some similarities between her case and your own, no rational person could possibly make such an accusation."

"They're still thinking it," she replied, close to tears.

"You need to reconsider -"

"No-one can make me!" she continued, glancing out the window and spotting a couple of police officers approaching the house. "Looks like it's time for the lunchtime update," she muttered, wiping a couple of tears from her cheek. "I don't mind therapy for general shitty life stuff, but I'm not going deeper, I'm not going back into the past. I feel like someone's doing all of this on purpose, just to force me, like they think they can break me if they force me to relive the whole damn thing."

"What are you scared of, Charlotte?" Dr. Gould asked.

"Nothing."

"Are you sure?" He paused. "Are you absolutely certain that this current event isn't prompting you to start remembering things that you'd previously suppressed?"

She opened her mouth to reply, but no words came out.

"Have you still not told your family that you've sought therapy?"

"I..." She paused.

"I've always been very clear," Dr. Gould continued, "that if you ever want our sessions to dig back into -"

"I don't," she said firmly.

"Are you sure?"

"Absolutely," she replied, even though there was the faintest hint of doubt in her mind. "It's other people. They're talking about me, and thinking about me -"

"There's that paranoia again," Dr. Gould pointed out with infuriating calmness. "Charlotte, you have to calm down and consider coming back to London immediately. Are you under suspicion of being involved in your niece's disappearance?"

"Suspicion?" she paused. "My sister seems -"

"I'm talking about the police," he replied, interrupting her. "Have the police advised you that they have any reason to suspect your involvement?"

"No," she said, "of course not."

"Provided you're free to leave," he continued, "I think you should get back to London as fast as possible. I believe you're at risk of suffering significant mental harm if you stay in that house a moment longer."

"I can't just leave," she replied. "She's still missing! I can't leave Ruth."

"Because she's your sister?"

"Because she's my sister."

"There's nothing you can do to help find the missing girl," he replied. "Nothing! You have to let the police do their job, Charlotte, and you have to let me do mine. I can't force you, but I'm advising you very strongly to remove yourself from such a damaging situation." He paused, as if he was waiting for her to meekly acquiesce. "I don't mean to alarm you," he added, "but even in this short phone conversation, you'd said a number of things that give me cause for concern. You don't sound like yourself."

"Of course I'm myself," she muttered, before pausing as she stared out the window. Her mind was churning, racing with possibilities, but while she could actually bring herself to consider leaving both Ruth and her mother, she couldn't contemplate abandoning Sophie. "I need to be here a little longer," she said eventually. "Even if it's bad for me, I need to stay and make sure that..." She paused again, trying to work out why she felt so strongly that she couldn't leave. "It's Sophie," she added, close to tears. "That poor little girl doesn't deserve anything like this. What if someone's taken her? What if someone's abducted her?"

"That's probably what has happened," Dr. Gould replied.

"Don't say that," Charlotte whimpered, shocked by his coldness.

"I'm just being honest with you," he continued. "If she's been missing for twenty-four hours and there's no sign of a body in the river, then the most likely explanation is an abduction."

Charlotte took a deep breath. She usually appreciated Dr. Gould's honesty, but right now she couldn't bear the thought of Sophie being held captive by some kind of monstrous... She closed her eyes, feeling as if fear was gripping her entire body. Having for so long prided herself on remaining in control of her emotions, she now felt that she was losing her grip.

"How do you think you would react," Dr. Gould continued slowly, "if -"

"I have to go," Charlotte said, hearing raised voices downstairs. "Something's kicking off."

"But Charlotte, how -"

"Got to go," she said again, before disconnecting the call. It sounded as if Ruth and Tony were arguing in the kitchen, and Charlotte couldn't help thinking that even though her sister was suffering, she seemed to be taking her pain out on everyone around her. Then again, Charlotte had to acknowledge that she didn't really understand how it felt to be a mother. This was the one area where Ruth was the expert, and Charlotte recognized that she couldn't really compete. She'd never been more aware of the fact that she lacked experience regarding children. Not only had she never had any of her own, but she barely even remembered being one.

***

"They're going to find her," Tony was saying as Charlotte arrived at the kitchen door a few minutes later. Leaning over his wife, who was sitting slumped at the kitchen table, he seemed fraught and tired, as if most of the strings holding him up had already been cut. "The hardest part is hanging onto hope," he continued, running a hand over Ruth's back. "The really hard part -"

"Do you want to know the hardest part?" Ruth replied suddenly, looking up at her husband with tear-filled, scornful eyes. "The hardest part is carrying a child for nine months, giving birth to her, raising her for eight years and then having her vanish one day like she never even -"

Before she could finish, Ruth spotted Charlotte and fell silent.

"Any news?" Charlotte asked after a moment.

"What do *you* think?" Ruth asked, wiping tears from her cheeks. "Of course there's no fucking news."

"Does anyone want a cup of tea?" Charlotte asked, making her way to the kettle.

"Thanks," Tony muttered.

"No!" Ruth said firmly. "Don't touch anything!"

Charlotte turned to her.

"This isn't your house," Ruth continued. "That's not your kettle or your tea, so why the hell do you presume to start offering things to people?"

"I just wanted to help," Charlotte said quietly.

"If you can't help me find my daughter," Ruth continued, with pure hatred in her voice, "then what's the fucking point of you?"

"Sweetheart -" Tony started to say.

"No!" Ruth shouted, pushing him aside before getting to her feet and advancing upon Charlotte. "What are you, anyway?" she continued. "A sister? You've never been a proper sister, not since your little year away. You're just some barren, sarcastic whore who keeps turning up in my life to make fun of me!" With tears in her eyes, Ruth paused for a moment, breathless after her outburst. "I hate you," she said finally, with sudden calm in her voice. "I've lost my daughter, who I love more than anything or anyone in the world, and yet my bitch of a sister is still here. I'd give anything to change that. Anything."

Charlotte opened her mouth to reply, but once again no words came out.

"Maybe you should have a rest," Tony said, putting an arm on Ruth's shoulder.

"Not while this bitch is in my house," Ruth sneered.

"It's okay," Charlotte said, "I'm going." With that, she turned and hurried through to the hallway, filled with the need to get as far away from the house, and from Ruth, as possible.

"She's just upset," Tony said, coming through to watch as she put her shoes on and grabbed her coat.

"I'm sure Sophie'll come back soon," Charlotte replied, hoping that by not looking directly at her brother-in-law she might be able to hide the tears in her eyes. She just wanted to get to her car and get the hell away from everyone. "If the police need anything," she continued, opening the door, "just give them my details and tell them to get in touch. I don't think there's anything else I can do here."

"Wait," Tony said, hurrying over and giving her an unexpected hug. "Please don't leave," he whispered, his lips close to her ear. "I need someone else sane in the house."

Charlotte shook her head.

"Please," Tony continued, still holding her in the hug, as if he was trying to prevent her from leaving. "I think it's going to be like it was with you, and I don't know how Ruth and I are going to handle that."

"What do you mean?" Charlotte asked, waiting for him to release her.

"It might be a year before she comes back," Tony replied. "Like with you."

Charlotte closed her eyes. In that split second, she realized two things. First, that Tony had given up hope of Sophie suddenly turning up, and second, that he'd begun to cling to the idea that somehow the miracle of twenty years earlier would be repeated. Charlotte wanted to tell him that he was wrong, to explain that he was making a mistake, but she couldn't bring herself to say the words.

"She's just scared," Tony said, finally releasing Charlotte from the hug. There were tears in his eyes now, and he looked deathly pale, even sick. "She doesn't mean the things she says."

"If I thought staying would help find Sophie," Charlotte replied, "I'd do it. But..." She paused. "I'll just go back to London for a few days, sort some things out and..." She took a deep breath. She knew she was being a bad sister by leaving, but at the same time, she couldn't stand to be around Ruth's venomous bile. "I'll be back," she said finally, even though she was planning to stay away. "I promise. I'll be back to help out, but I need to go and sort some things out. Okay?"

Tony paused. "Okay," he said finally, although it was clear that he didn't really believe her.

"I promise," Charlotte lied. "I'll be back in a few days." With that, she turned and walked out the door, and although she didn't look back, she knew that Tony was watching her leave. She was tempted to turn back, to ease her brother-in-law's burden by agreeing to stay, but she'd already made a decision that required her to leave. Rattling around the house, arguing incessantly with her sister, wouldn't bring Sophie back. But she had an idea that *might*.

***

"Are you sure about this?" Dr. Gould said hesitantly.

Charlotte took a deep breath. She'd driven a half-mile from her sister's home before parking up at the side of the road and making the phone call she'd never, ever thought she'd make.

"I'm sure," she said, her voice tense and tearless.

"Is this because of your niece?"

"Yes."

"And you're aware that no matter what progress we might make in your case, there's no -"

"I know," she said, cutting him off. "It probably won't help Sophie, but it *might*. And even if there's only a one in a million chance, and even if it opens up a whole lot of bad memories for me, I want to do it. Do you think it's possible?"

Dr. Gould paused for a moment. "I've always felt that the memories are buried deep within your subconscious mind," he said eventually, "but that with patient work, we might be able to retrieve at least some of them." He paused again. "There are no guarantees, Charlotte, but I think we should be able to get somewhere."

"I'll be back in London by tonight," she replied, "so when can you fit me in?"

"We'll start tomorrow," he replied calmly. "I'll schedule you for an extra session at five, is that okay?"

"Five," Charlotte said, staring straight ahead. "I'll be there."

"And Charlotte," he continued, "please try to... retain some perspective. It's a good thing, in my opinion, that you're willing to take this step in your own life, but I highly doubt that it's going to resolve anything in terms of whatever fate has befallen your niece."

"I know," she replied, as tears welled up in her eyes again, "but I have to try. For Sophie's sake."

"I'll see you tomorrow at five," Dr. Gould replied.

Charlotte opened her mouth to reply, but no words came out. Instead, she was suddenly hit by an uncontrollable wave of grief that crashed through her body and reduced her to a sobbing, bawling wreck. Letting her head drop to her chest, she closed her eyes and tried in vain to pull herself together, but eventually all that came out were a series of loud sobs.

"Charlotte?" Dr. Gould said after a moment. "Are you okay?"

She cut the call off and dropped the phone onto the passenger seat before leaning forward and resting her head on the steering wheel. Waves of fear and pain swept through her, and for several minutes she could do nothing but sob uncontrollably until, finally, she felt that she was going to throw up. She lost track of time for a while, but eventually the sobbing started to subside and she opened her eyes and looked out the window.

She sat in trembling silence for a moment, as the last tears rolled down her cheeks.

"Where are you?" she whispered, staring out at the miles of rolling fields and forest. "Where the hell are you?"

One year later

Part Three

Drowning

Today

At first it was just a faint sound in the middle of the night, a kind of scratching noise, as if a tree branch was being blown against the window. It was enough to briefly disturb Charlotte's sleep, causing her to roll onto her side. For a few minutes, the sound seemed to abate, before coming back with renewed vigor, scratching incessantly on the glass until Charlotte's eyes flicked open. She was still half-asleep, but she was beginning to become aware that something was wrong.

The room was pitch black, with just the faintest hint of moonlight picking out the edges of the window. Charlotte remained perfectly still, her tired eyes watching the darkness and listening as the scratching sound faded away for a few minutes. Just as she was about to try going back to sleep, however, Charlotte realized she could hear it again, and this time it seemed less like a tree branch and more like... She couldn't help but imagine small fingers, their nails scratching against the outside of the window frame, and this immediately brought Charlotte all the way out of her slumber. She stared into the darkness and listened as the scratching became more of a rubbing sound, and finally she realized that for her own peace of mind, she'd have to go and check that nothing was wrong.

Pushing the duvet aside, she swung her legs over the side of the bed and sat in silence for a moment, watching the window. Her mind raced as she tried to work out whether there were any trees in the little alley that ran along the side of her apartment, but she was fairly sure that there was nothing out there that should be making such a noise. Getting to her feet, she tried to tell herself that the culprit must be a mouse, or perhaps a bird with a twig in its mouth. As she picked her way across the dark room, her bare feet brushing against piles of discarded clothing, she came up with dozens of increasingly outlandish explanations for the noise: she imagined a variety of birds, rodents, squirrels, foxes, badgers, hedgehogs... pretty much any kind of animal native to the British Isles, she considered might be out on the window ledge, making the noise.

Placing her hand on the latch, she put her face close to the glass for a moment, just to make sure that there wasn't a burglar out there, waiting to pounce.

She took a deep breath before finally opening the lock and pushing the window open. Leaning out, she felt a gust of cold air hit her naked torso as she looked down at the alley below. A nearby streetlight illuminated the scene with an electric orange glow, enough to show that there seemed to be neither man nor beast in the area. Looking around and then up, Charlotte made doubly sure that there was nothing to see, and only then did she allow herself to consider the possibility that the scratching sound had all been part of a dream that had maybe lingered a few seconds longer than usual. She looked down at her arms and saw that she was getting chicken skin from the cold, so she pulled the window shut and made doubly sure to close the latch so that -

Suddenly a shape loomed toward her from the other side of the window and smashed the glass, showering her with shards as a small arm reached through and grabbed her wrist. Startled, Charlotte stepped back and tried to get free of the child's grip, before a small face appeared from the darkness, staring at her. For a fraction of a second, she thought that it was Sophie, before realizing that it was someone she'd never seen before; as the child reached another hand toward her, Charlotte panicked and tried to push the girl away, her fingers pressing against the visitor's ice-cold face. Finally, in an act of sheer desperation, she forced the girl down onto the shards of broken glass at the bottom of the window, instantly skewering the child's neck. As she adjusted her grip, Charlotte realized that cold blood was flowing over her hands from the gash in the girl's flesh, but as she tried to get free, she succeeded only in slicing the girl against the rest of the glass until blood was pouring from the wound.

"Get off!" Charlotte shouted, putting both her hands on the girl's face and pushing with all her strength. There was a loud ripping sound, like some kind of cloth canvas being torn, and the girl's head tilted back, exposing the stump of her neck caught on a sharp piece of glass. Charlotte tried to call out again, but suddenly she felt as if her lungs were full of water. For a moment, the meat of the girl's neck glistened in the faint moonlight, before Charlotte - caught up in a blind panic - pushed one final time and fell from the girl's grasp, landing on the bed and rolling over just in time to come face to face with the panicked stare of the guy who had been trying to sleep next to her.

"Charlotte?" he said. "What's wrong?"

She turned and looked back at the window, but the light seemed different now and it was clear that the glass was unbroken. Still trying to catch her breath, Charlotte sat up and looked at her hands, finding that there was no blood. She paused for a moment, before turning to the guy and realizing with sudden clarity that it wasn't just 'some guy' at all. It was John, and he was *supposed* to be in her bed. In fact, he'd been in her bed every night for the past six months.

"Nightmare?" he asked, looking startled.

Charlotte paused. The experience with the young girl had seemed so real and so vivid, she found it impossible to accept that the whole thing could have been a simple nightmare. Then again, there was no other possible explanation, and so she forced herself to accept that, somehow, it had all been in her mind.

"You okay?" John asked, handing her a glass of water from his bedside table. "Charlotte?"

"I'm fine," she replied, taking a sip. "I warned you I might be a little..." Her voice trailed off as she replayed the image of the girl's face over and over again. It wasn't Sophie, in fact it wasn't anyone she recognized, but those two little dark eyes had stared at her with such intensity, she couldn't get them out of her mind. She could still feel the girl's ice-cold hands on her skin, and she was convinced that at any moment the vision would come back.

"Do you want to talk about it?" John asked.

She turned to him. "No," she said after a few seconds. "I mean, it was just a nightmare, right? It was just..." She paused. "It was just a dream."

"Sure," John replied, clearly aware that he shouldn't press any further. "Maybe we shouldn't have cheese so close to bed, huh?"

"Maybe," Charlotte replied, trying to force herself to smile. She'd successfully avoided telling John about the worst of her past since they'd first met six months ago. He knew that her niece had gone missing, of course, but other than that she'd been remarkably, skillfully vague. Most people would probably have tied themselves into knots with all the half-truths and omissions she'd been forced to deploy, but Charlotte had always been very good at mental gymnastics, and she salved her conscience by telling herself that it was for his own good that he was kept in the dark. It helped, too, that she'd had no contact with her sister since the day she left the house almost exactly a year earlier.

"Come here," John said, putting a large, well-toned arm around her.

Charlotte hated herself for being so easy to console, but she had to admit that John's embrace always made her feel better. She'd never taken herself to be the kind of woman who could get all giddy in the arms of a strong man, and in fact she'd laughed at that kind of woman in the past; right now, however, she just wanted John to hold her as she sat and stared at the window, convinced that the little girl's image was going to come back at any moment.

"Sleepy time?" he asked, kissing her shoulder.

Charlotte nodded, but as she settled down and turned her back on John, allowing him to spoon her, she couldn't shake the memory of the girl's face. If it had been Sophie who had appeared in her nightmares, she could almost understand how and why her subconscious mind might be trying to torture her. This girl, however, had been a complete stranger, and it was the lack of recognition that gave Charlotte the most trouble. Given the amount of crap that she'd already been through, why did her mind want to *invent* new stuff? Closing her eyes, she tried to get some sleep, although she knew deep down that she'd be awake until morning.

Today

"Have you been thinking about the past a lot recently?" Dr. Gould asked as he sat behind his desk, making notes in his ledger. "With the anniversary coming up, it would be natural for you to have your niece's disappearance on your mind."

Charlotte paused, wondering what to say. She thought about Sophie at least half a dozen times every day, so it was hard to know whether she was giving the girl more consideration than usual. "Maybe," she said eventually, feeling hopelessly out of her depth. It was as if these sessions with Dr. Gould always reminded her how little control she had over her own mind.

"Maybe's not an answer," he replied. "Let me try to put the question to you in another way. Are you frustrated by our lack of progress?"

She nodded.

"Do you think that this is *your* failing? Or maybe mine?"

"I guess you know what you're doing," Charlotte replied.

"And yet whenever we try to trace a route back into your childhood," he continued, "we reach a brick wall."

"Not a brick wall," she pointed out. "Just... nothing."

"You must have been a child once," he replied with a faint smile. "You were eight years old when you disappeared, Charlotte, and nine when you reappeared. You must have existed during that year when you were gone, just as you must have existed when you were a young girl, but none of it seems to be stored in your mind. It's as if, in whatever way and for whatever reason, you've done an extremely good job of blocking much of your childhood from your memory." He paused. "What about your father? Did you do the exercises I set for you?"

"I couldn't," she replied.

"Why not?"

"Well..." She paused. "I tried to think back to what he was like," she continued after a moment, "but I was kinda just... making it up. I ended up writing down stuff about how I wanted him to be, rather than how he actually was. And then the part about looking at photos..." She took a deep breath. "I only have one photo of him, and when I look at it, I might as well be staring at a perfect stranger."

"During our last session, you said you were going to contact your sister and ask for some different photos."

"I said *maybe* I'd contact my sister," she replied.

"When it comes to you," he continued, "I rather feel that 'maybe' is a code word. It's a way of refusing while simultaneously trying to avoid an argument."

Charlotte sighed.

"So *did* you talk to her?"

She shook her head.

"Why not?"

"It's difficult," she replied. "Things are... awkward between us. Trust me, she was like the queen bitch even before all of this happened."

"But she's lost her only child," Dr. Gould countered. "Doesn't that make you want to be with her? Even if she's difficult, even if she's a *queen bitch* as you put it, isn't it just basic human compassion to go and support a family member who's going through such trauma?" He waited for an answer. "Don't you feel anything for her?"

Charlotte paused. The truth was, she hated the idea of seeing Ruth again, and she was quite happy with the thought that she might not ever have to go back to that goddamn house again. At the same time, she knew that eventually she'd *have* to return. After all, she couldn't just abandon the woman, even if she was still sensitive from some of the things that Ruth had said when they'd last been together.

"Charlotte?" Dr. Gould continued. "I asked you a question. Do you feel anything for your sister?"

"Maybe," she replied.

"Maybe?"

She paused. "Maybe."

"And have you thought about the other matter that we discussed?"

A faint smile crept onto Charlotte's lips.

"You haven't told your sister about your good news?"

"I'm still not sure I believe it myself," Charlotte replied. "John and I have only been going out for..." She paused. "I always thought it couldn't happen to me. Hell, I didn't get my first period until I was nineteen, for God's sake, and then... I really thought I was barren. It's kinda weird to think that I could..." Her voice trailed off, and it was as if she couldn't quite get the words out of her mouth.

"I think you should tell your sister," Dr. Gould said after a moment.

"Maybe," she replied.

"Maybe?"

She took a deep breath. "Maybe. Some day."

***

"Are you coming?" Tony asked, his voice sounding a little crackly on the phone. "Ruth says she sent you a few emails, but you haven't replied."

Walking along the busy London street, Charlotte silently rued her weakness in answering the call. If it had been Ruth trying to get in touch, she could have easily ignored the persistent buzzing in her bag, but Tony was another matter. Charlotte liked Tony, or at least she felt sorry for him, and she figured the poor guy at least deserved an answer.

"Maybe."

"Please, Charlotte. It'd mean a lot to both of us."

"I'm not sure I can make *this* weekend," she said, stopping on a corner and putting a finger in one ear so that she could hear him better. "I'm kinda rushed off my -"

"It'll be one year on Saturday," Tony said, his voice sounding tense, lending extra meaning to such a simple and innocent statement.

"I know," Charlotte replied cautiously, picking her words with care. "I know that, but -"

"I think it'd be good to have everyone here," Tony continued. "It's been a while since your last visit, and..." He paused, and suddenly it seemed as if there was a trace of excitement in his words, as if he was anticipating some kind of big revelation. "You know it's possible, right?" he asked eventually. "It'd be good to have you here, either way."

Charlotte paused. There was no way she wanted to go back to that house, especially not for some kind of anniversary pantomime. She knew full well that there was no way Sophie was going to show up, but at the same time, there was a part of her that wanted to be there for the moment of proof.

"Are you still there?" Tony asked.

"Yeah," Charlotte replied, feeling as if there was a lump in her throat. "It's just that work -"

"You don't think she'll come, do you?"

Charlotte winced. The poor guy was clearly filled with hope. "I'm, er..." She paused, trying desperately to think of a way to get out of the commitment.

"Please," he said plaintively.

"Maybe next weekend?"

"*This* weekend is the anniversary," he replied. "On Saturday, it will have been exactly a year since Sophie disappeared. I think... I think you *need* to be here, you know? For it to happen?"

Charlotte took a deep breath as she realized that Tony seemed to have bought hook, line and sinker into the whole ludicrous idea. It was as if, in some strange way, the poor guy felt that her presence was required in order for some mystical, magical event to take place. The last thing Charlotte wanted was to encourage such a ridiculous idea, but at the same time, she felt as if there was no way she could turn Tony down so flatly. There was also a small part of her that felt she'd be abandoning Sophie if she didn't at least go and mark the anniversary of her disappearance.

"I can't make it on Friday," she said eventually, hating herself for each word, "but maybe I could drive up there on Saturday morning -"

"Saturday's fine," Tony said quickly, as if he was snatching her acquiescence before she could change her mind. "I'll make sure the spare room's made up for you, and we'll put on a big dinner, and..." He paused. "Out of interest, Charlotte, and I hope you don't mind me asking, but when you came back all those years ago... what time of day did it happen?"

Charlotte paused. "I don't know," she said eventually. "You'd have to ask Ruth or my mother.""

"I'm just trying to plan ahead," Tony continued with an embarrassed laugh. "You know, on the off-chance. I know it's probably *not* going to happen that way, but I suppose we should cover all the eventualities, shouldn't we? Just in case there's some kind of miracle."

"You know -"

"So we'll have a big dinner to celebrate," he added, cutting her off before she could pour cold water on his plans. "I'll roast a duck or something. Really push the boat out, you know? I'm sure Ruth'll be pleased to have you back here, and your mother has been asking after you in her own inimitable way." He paused. "I should probably be straight up with you and warn you, Charlotte. Helen's not doing so good. That's another reason why I think you should come. Her moments of confusion are getting worse, and her periods of lucidity are kind of fleeting these days. If you stay away much longer..."

She waited for him to finish, but she already knew how the conversation was going to end. So far, she'd gone from refusal to lying agreement, and now it was time to say the words she'd been putting off for a year. "Sure," she said, inwardly hating herself, "I'll come down on Saturday and stay until Sunday. I need to be back on Sunday night, 'cause I've got work the next morning, but..." She paused again. "I'll come," she said, as if to reaffirm the idea in her own mind. "I promise."

"Ruth'll be so pleased," Tony replied.

"Liar."

"I think you'll be surprised," he continued. "She's mellowed. I think it's because..." He paused. "Well, you know, the anniversary is coming up, and I guess stranger things have happened before."

"I'll see you on Saturday," Charlotte replied, preferring to cut the mystical bullshit. "I should be there around lunchtime."

Once the call was over, she found herself desperately trying to think of a way she could back out without making it seem painfully obvious that she was trying to avoid her sister. The last thing she wanted to do was sit around that house and wait while everyone else wondered whether or not Sophie might follow her lead by making a sudden, miraculous reappearance. All she could think about was the fact that after a year of waiting and hoping, the fact of Sophie's disappearance was about to be firmly, finally put to rest. She just hoped that, wherever she was and whatever had happened to her, the poor girl hadn't suffered.

Today

It hadn't changed, Charlotte realized as she parked outside the house. The world had swung around the sun since her last visit, and four seasons had left subtle marks, but for the most part the old brick house looked exactly the same as before.

"Damn it," she muttered, drumming her fingers nervously on the steering wheel. "Why am I such a fucking nice person?"

The front door opened before Charlotte was even out of the car. With a nervous smile on his face, Tony looked desperately relieved to see that she'd finally shown up. He was wearing a particularly jaunty jumper, bright red with unseasonal brown reindeer marching in a procession across his chest. Charlotte couldn't help but wonder if he'd had to put away his more colorful jumpers for a period following Sophie's disappearance, as a mark of respect.

"Smell that?" Tony said with a theatrical sniff as he hurried out and grabbed Charlotte's backpack from her hands. "A whole roast duck, bathing in its own juices, seasoned and timed to perfection by hands that have completed several cooking classes."

"Sounds good," Charlotte said, giving him a limp hug while glancing at the house, which seemed pregnant with the promise of Ruth's presence. Somewhere in that stone building, Charlotte's stone sister was waiting, and the question was whether she'd have mellowed over the past year, or whether she'd pick up the sisters' argument right where they'd left it a year ago. Somehow, Charlotte suspected the latter.

"Anything I should know?" she asked as Tony led her to the front door.

"Dinner's ready at five," he replied jovially, clearly being careful to step around the big questions.

Charlotte smiled politely as she entered the house, and she was immediately assaulted by familiar smells: her mother's perfume, unchanged for decades; her sister's favorite fruit tea; and Tony's roast duck, a family staple for many years. It was as if the smells wrapped themselves around Charlotte and mocked her as they welcomed her back.

As soon as she heard footsteps in one of the upstairs rooms, Charlotte tensed. Seconds later, Ruth appeared at the top of the stairs and came hurrying down, with a highly uncharacteristic smile on her face. She immediately swung her arms around Charlotte, giving her the kind of hug that people usually reserve for those whose company they actually enjoy. It was a strange, elongated moment that Charlotte felt must be some kind of trap, but as the hug continued, the whole thing began to feel more and more sincere.

Definitely a trap, then.

"I'm so glad you came," Ruth said eventually, taking a step back. "You look..." She paused, her eyes alive with a bright smile. "I was going to say you look healthier or happier or older or wiser or... some such bollocks, but the truth is, you look exactly the same. It's like it was only yesterday that you walked out the door." Grabbing her by the arm, she led Charlotte through to the front room, but not before Charlotte was able to register her shock with a well-timed glance back at Tony, who simply shrugged.

"Where's Mum?" Charlotte asked, stunned by the rapturous reception she was receiving.

"Having a nap," Ruth replied, and for the first time since Charlotte's arrival, her smile was interrupted by a fleeting moment of sadness. "I'll fill you in later. But come on," she added, leading her over to the patio doors and out onto the porch overlooking the lawn, "tell me what's been going on in your life. It's been far too long. Tony'll bring us a drink each before he starts buttering his duck. God, there's a sentence I never thought I'd say."

Charlotte smiled politely. She'd prepared for every possible welcome: she'd been ready to have things thrown at her; she'd been ready for the silent treatment; she'd been ready for bitter, muttered asides or possibly even a balls-to-the-wall slanging match. The one thing she *hadn't* been prepared for - in fact, the one thing she'd never even considered -

was a friendly, pleasant conversation over drinks. She felt strangely friendly toward her sister, although she was still considering the possibility that the whole thing was a trap. As they approached the deckchairs, she took a quick look around the base of hers before sitting down, just in case it had been placed over a trapdoor.

"I was wrong," Ruth said as she sat down. "You *don't* look the same. You look healthy, Charlotte."

Charlotte smiled. She was so flabbergasted, she wasn't quite sure where to start, but she wasn't ready to tell Ruth about her tentative relationship with John, or any of her other news. Not yet, anyway. She felt, in a way, that admitting to happy news would be tantamount to admitting that Ruth was right about life.

"You know," she said eventually, with an evasive smile as she couldn't help but glance toward the river, "London's busy. *Very* busy. Lots of people, lots of things to do." She paused, realizing that her sister was listening with rapt attention. "Lots of stuff," she added uncomfortably. "Um, lots of... nights out. Lots of long days at work. Lots of -"

"Lots of everything, from the sounds of it," Ruth said, still smiling as Tony placed a couple of drinks on the little table between them. "Vodka and orange," she added. "I know it's early, but it's Saturday, so what the hell?" Grabbing the drink, she held it up toward Charlotte. "Cheers!"

"Cheers," Charlotte replied, picking up her drink but merely raising it to her lips for a moment before putting it back down untouched.

"You don't like vodka and orange anymore?" Ruth asked.

"I'll wait a bit."

"Just let us know if you'd rather have something else," Ruth continued. "We've got the spirits cabinet pretty well-stocked these days."

Charlotte took a deep breath. It was as if aliens had landed, scooped up the real Ruth, and replaced her with some kind of copy; they'd managed to get the physical appearance down pat, but they'd completely messed up the personality and had accidentally made this new version of Ruth seem overly happy and friendly. Having a normal, cheerful conversation with Ruth was about as normal as watching an elephant perform ballet, and Charlotte felt bad for not being able to properly relax.

"So Mummy's getting worse," Ruth said after a moment, with a hint of sadness in her eyes. "*Much* worse. She drifts in and out of these clouds of dementia, but most of the time she'd too far gone to really..." She paused. "She keeps talking as if Daddy's around, for one thing, which is mildly infuriating during the day and downright creepy late at night. She seems to be retreating into the undamaged parts of her brain, but there aren't proper connections between those parts so she ends up trapped in these little loops until, occasionally, a little misfire sends her across the void to another bubble. It's quite frightening, really, but totally manageable. She's less trouble, and at least she's still toilet-trained. Still, we're going to have to put her in a home."

"Really?" Charlotte replied, shocked at the idea.

"Of course," Ruth continued. "She simply can't stay here. Tony and I can handle her, to some extent, but she's going to..." She paused. "Look, the truth is, and I feel bad for saying this, but I can't have Mummy around Sophie. An unstable old woman isn't good for a child, and it's only going to get worse. I should have made the decision before today, really, but I think the best thing for everyone would be to find a nice, friendly residential home where Mummy can make some new friends. People her own age, you know? People with the same interests and problems."

Charlotte stared at her sister, unable to quite untangle the sentences she just heard.

"What's wrong?" Ruth replied with a nervous smile. "You look like you've seen a ghost."

"No," Charlotte said, "it's just..."

"I know it's a shock," Ruth continued, "and believe me, I've wrestled with my conscience. But I can't let Mummy scare Sophie, can I? I'm sure the old dear would understand, if she was capable of understanding anything. I'll just have to break the news to Sophie gently, and hope that she's able to understand that this is no-one's fault."

Charlotte paused. "Um..." She paused again. "Ruth?" Another pause. "When you say... Sophie?" She paused yet again as she tried to work out what was happening. Glancing back at the house, she could see Tony hard at work in the kitchen.

"What's wrong?" Ruth asked. "You seem confused?"

"You keep mentioning Sophie," Charlotte replied, turning to her. "I was meaning to ask -"

"Now that she's coming back," Ruth continued, "we have to take her needs into account. The past year has been difficult with Mummy, but Tony and I are adults and we can handle it. Sophie's a different kettle of fish, though, isn't she? She's still so young and impressionable."

"Sophie's coming back?" Charlotte asked, her heart racing. Again, she turned to look at the house.

"Of course," Ruth replied, as if it was the most natural thing in the world. "Today's the one year anniversary of her disappearance, silly."

"Yes, but -" Charlotte turned back to her. "But..."

"Today's the one year anniversary," Ruth replied with a grin, "so she'll be coming back today." She checked her watch. "God knows what time, though. Do you happen to know what time you returned all those years ago? Was it the same time you disappeared? I suppose we've got until midnight, but I'd prefer to get her back before dinner."

Her heart starting to sink, Charlotte stared at her sister for a moment and suddenly realized that there was, after all, something dark hidden behind that grin. Maybe not dark, exactly, but desperate and tragic. As she glanced back at the house again, Charlotte briefly made eye contact with Tony, and they shared a look that made it abundantly clear that Ruth's behavior was nothing to celebrate.

"I'm so glad you came today," Ruth said, leaning over and rubbing Charlotte's knee before turning to take a sip of her drink and watch the gate at the far end of the lawn. "I've been waiting so long for this day, Charlotte. The day Sophie does what you did and comes back from wherever she's been."

Today

"You didn't tell me she was a fucking nut-case!" Charlotte hissed a few hours later, standing in the kitchen while Tony served up the roast duck.

"I thought that was assumed," he replied, carefully ladling out the juices from the tin. "Hasn't that been standard policy in your family for decades?"

"She thinks Sophie's coming back!" Charlotte continued, glancing at the door to make sure that Ruth was still busy setting the table in the dining room.

Tony put the tin down on the draining board. "Careful of that," he muttered, "it's hot."

"She needs to see a fucking psychiatrist," Charlotte replied, keeping her voice down. "What the hell are you going to say to her when it gets to midnight and Sophie doesn't reappear?"

Tony shrugged.

"Haven't you thought of that?" Charlotte asked, stunned by her brother-in-law's apparent lack of care. After a moment, however, the pieces started to fall into place and she sighed as she watched Tony portion out the potatoes. "Oh fucking Christ," she muttered. "Jesus fucking Christ. You're both..."

Tony ignored her, focusing instead on the food.

"You think she's right, don't you?" Charlotte continued, suddenly struck by the tragedy of the house. "You both think Sophie's going to come back today."

"You don't know that she isn't," Tony replied, placing a couple of slices of roast duck on each plate. "So far, Sophie's disappearance has been exactly like yours, and we all know how that turned out, don't we?" He took a step back and admired his work. "I shot this duck myself, you know," he added, clearly keen to change the subject. "Don't worry, though. There won't be any lead in the carcass. I've cooked duck... Gosh, it must be hundreds of times over the years, and I've never got any lead in there yet."

"Shut the fuck up about your fucking duck," Charlotte muttered as she realized that, far from coming back to a house that had come to terms with its tragedy, she'd wandered straight into the middle of a nightmare. "Why isn't she pregnant?" she asked suddenly. "You need to move on, Tony. You need to get past everything that happened! You need..." She paused, wondering whether she should say what she was thinking. "You need to have another child. Maybe a couple, you know? It won't replace Sophie, but it'll be a way to remind yourselves that life goes on."

"We're thinking of having more," he replied uncertainly. "We just wanted to wait until..." He paused. "Well, you know how it is, you need to do one thing at a time, don't you? We thought we should probably focus on Sophie first, and then maybe in a year or two we can start to think about some new additions to the family."

They stood in silence for a moment as Tony looked at the roast duck and Charlotte stared in shocked, open-mouthed horror at her brother-in-law. She found it hard to believe the fantasy world that Ruth and Tony had created, and she felt certain that it was going to come crashing down sooner or later. Probably sooner.

"You're going to break each other's hearts," she said after a moment, all her anger suddenly replaced by pity, and by the realization that everything would fall apart at midnight. "You're fucking idiots, do you know that?"

"Can you carry this plate through?" Tony asked, passing a plate to her. "I can manage the rest." He looked up at the ceiling as the wood creaked. "Great," he added, "sounds like Helen's smelled the food. I hope you enjoy the duck, Charlotte. I think it's my best yet."

Charlotte opened her mouth to argue with him, but she realized that she'd only be banging her head against a stone wall. It was as if a spell had been cast on her sister and brother-in-law, rendering them deaf to the rational world while they plunged deeper down a rabbit-hole of false hope. Although she was by no means opposed to self-delusion, Charlotte felt that this particular fantasy had a very clear sell-by date: by midnight, it would be abundantly clear that Sophie wasn't coming back, in which case Ruth and Tony would have to face the truth.

***

Dinner was delicious and sorrowful.

As she slowly made her way through her portion of duck, Charlotte didn't know where to look. Ruth was eating happily, chatting away to Tony about plans to maybe take a family holiday the next year, and between them they made for a pitiful sight. As if that wasn't bad enough, Charlotte and Ruth's mother Helen was sitting alone at the other side of the table, mournfully eating her food and keeping her head down, as if she was ashamed to be in polite company. There was also a spare place made up, clearly designed for Sophie in case the girl happened to reappear during dinner, while the patio door was open to let the air of a warm summer's evening into the house. Everything was set for Sophie's arrival, but there was one problem:

Charlotte knew full well that the little girl wouldn't be making an appearance.

After dinner, Tony suggested that everyone should sit out on the porch. The explanation given was that it'd be nice to have some sherry and enjoy the evening, but Charlotte knew that the real purpose was to have a perfect view of the lawn. As she slowly escorted her mother outside, Charlotte couldn't help but glance back at Ruth and Tony, who both had the same sad, forced smiles on their faces. It was almost nine o'clock, and there were only three hours to go before the day of Sophie's miraculous reappearance was going to come to an end. Charlotte had no idea how the couple would react when midnight arrived and Sophie was nowhere to be seen, but she'd already made a hard-hearted decision. In all likelihood, she'd jump into her car and drive through the night. She simply couldn't handle the emotional fallout of Ruth and Tony's mutual delusion.

"Mummy's very excited," Ruth said a few minutes later, as they all sat in a row, drinks in their hands. She leaned over and gave her mother's shoulder a reassuring pat. "You're not cold are you, Mummy?"

Ignoring her daughter, Helen kept her eyes firmly on the lawn. Her lower jaw was constantly trembling and the past year seemed to have made her eyes more milky than ever, while there was an air of fear about her face, as if she was terrified of the evening's events.

"Are you sure she's okay?" Charlotte whispered, leaning over to Ruth.

"Of course," Ruth replied with a smile. "Why wouldn't she be?"

"Her eyes," Charlotte continued. "Have you had her checked out? Are you sure she can see properly?"

"She's fine," Ruth replied.

"But she just -"

"She's fine," Ruth said again, a sliver of her old anger showing through for a moment. "She can see just fine." She paused, and the veil of good humor came down again, bringing the smile back to her face. "Stop worrying so much, Charlotte. Tonight's going to be a good night. Can't you feel it in your bones? It's going to be a really good, happy night."

Charlotte opened her mouth to argue with her, but suddenly she realized that her sister was close to tears. The effort required to believe something as fantastical as Sophie's impending return was clearly causing Ruth great strain, and although Charlotte wanted to find a way to help her sister, she finally leaned back in her chair, afraid to say or do anything. Instead, she watched as strands of late-night mist drifted slowly across the lawn.

"It's a lovely evening," Tony said after a few minutes. "Really... lovely."

"Yes," Ruth continued, her eyes fixed firmly on the gate at the far end of the garden. "So lovely."

Charlotte looked down at her vodka and orange. It was so damn tempting, but she knew she couldn't have any.

"Have you gone off the booze?" Tony asked with a nervous laugh. "Normally you'd be downing those things."

"I'm trying to cut back," Charlotte replied with a faint smile. "That's all."

The evening continued to drag past in excruciatingly slow fashion. Ruth and Tony made polite, jovial conversation, occasionally dragging Charlotte in to mutter a few words, but as ten o'clock and then eleven o'clock ticked past, the tension in the air was becoming increasingly palpable. Charlotte couldn't help but keep glancing over at her mother, whose expression had remained unchanged throughout: scared but stoical, the old woman didn't seem to have averted her gaze from the lawn once.

After a while, the polite chatter between Ruth and Tony died down, and when she checked her watch, Charlotte saw that there were only ten minutes left until midnight. She glanced at her sister and saw a look of concern on her face, due no doubt to the fact that soon the day's fantasy would be over. Although she wanted to leap up, grab Ruth and shake her until she realized the error of her ways, Charlotte felt frozen in place, as if she was too scared to get involved in anything that was happening. She wanted to just stay back, avoid drawing attention to herself, and hope against hope that perhaps she might not feel the full force of her sister's anger once the disappointment set in.

By one minute past midnight, they were all sitting in silence. It was as if no-one wanted to be the first to say anything, and Charlotte wondered whether Ruth and Tony planned to just sit out all night. Starting to feel cold and tired, she ached to go inside and draw the agonizing evening to a close, but she knew that if she so much as blinked, she'd be seen as the one who ended the family's hope. Staring at the gate at the far end of the lawn, she tried to imagine what it would have been like if Sophie *had* suddenly appeared. The joy would have been unbridled, the celebrations endless... and yet all that happiness could never be unleashed, because now it was painfully clear even to the most deluded family-members that Sophie was never, ever coming back.

"Well," Tony said after what felt like an eternity. "I don't know, maybe..." His voice trailed off, as if he was waiting for Ruth to give him a cue. "Would anyone like another drink?"

"I'll get them," Ruth said quickly, getting to her feet and grabbing the empty glasses before hurrying inside.

Charlotte glanced over at her brother-in-law and saw the fear in his eyes.

"This has to end," she whispered after a moment.

Tony nodded.

Getting to her feet, Charlotte made her way inside, but as soon as she got through to the kitchen, she realized she could hear someone sobbing. She walked over to the door and peered through to the darkened living room, where she saw Ruth standing in the shadows, a bottle of vodka in her hand as she wiped her eyes. It was such a private moment, Charlotte felt that even a sister had no right to intrude, so she hung back, wondering what to do next. She didn't want to just turn around and go back outside, but neither did she feel that she could leave her. Instead, she simply waited, half in the room and half out, half with her sister and half not, watching as Ruth slowly poured more drinks for them all. It was a sad, pathetic sight, and Charlotte couldn't help but wonder whether this was how her sister was going to live the rest of her life. With a steely heart, she realized that there was no way she was going to sit around and watch while -

Suddenly there was a cry from out on the porch. Charlotte turned, immediately recognizing the voice as her mother's.

"What was that?" Ruth asked, hurrying over to join her before turning to Charlotte. "Were you watching me?"

Ignoring her sister, Charlotte ran through to the other room and finally out onto the porch, where she found Tony desperately trying to support her mother while the old woman struggled forward, trying to make her way onto the lawn. It was as if, after a whole evening of inactivity, Helen had suddenly been spurred to push forward toward some goal that no-one else could see.

"Here," Charlotte said, grabbing her mother's arm and trying to pull her up. "Jesus, Mum. What the -"

Before she could finish, she heard the sound of glass smashing behind her. Turning, she saw Ruth standing in the doorway with a stunned look on her face, her glass having slipped from her hand.

"You gonna help?" Charlotte asked, before turning back to her mother and then glancing over at the lawn.

And that's when she saw it.

Still struggling to keep her flailing mother upright, Charlotte nevertheless couldn't take her eyes off the sight down by the gate at the far end of the garden. It was a dark night, with precious little moonlight, and there were still lines of mist drifting across the lawn, but as Charlotte stared in awestruck horror, she realized that there was an unmistakable figure outlined against the trees, standing down by the gate.

It was the silhouette of a little girl.

Today

"Sophie!" Ruth screamed, racing across the porch and almost knocking Charlotte and her mother over in the process. Steadying herself against the railing, Charlotte made sure her mother was upright before turning to watch as Ruth ran across the lawn.

"Sophie!" her sister shouted again, heading straight for the silhouette.

"Hold her," Tony said, shifting Helen's weight fully onto Charlotte before letting go and running after his wife as she got closer and closer to the little girl's figure.

***

"Stay here," Charlotte said, trying not to be too forceful as she dumped her mother's frame into a chair.

"Sophie!" Ruth screamed in the distance, down at the bottom of the garden. "Sophie!"

"Stay. Here!" Charlotte said firmly, before turning and looking across the lawn. Despite the mist, she could just about make out Ruth and Tony's figures in the distance. Her heart pounding, Charlotte set off after them.

***

Racing across the lawn, already desperately out of breath thanks to her dozen-fags-a-day habit, Charlotte damn near slipped over several times on the damp grass.

"Sophie!" Ruth was shoutng over and over again, just a few meters up ahead. "Sophie! Sophie!"

"Where is she?" Charlotte shouted as she came to a halt, only to finally lose her balance as one of her feet slid through the mud, leaving her to slam down hard on her back. Getting up quickly, she wiped mud from her legs as she tried to work out what was happening. "Where is she?" she shouted.

***

"She was right here," Ruth said, her voice filled with panic as she stood on the other side of the fence, turning around in circles as she looked for some sign of her daughter. "She was right here!" she screamed.

"I'm not sure," Tony said breathlessly. "I thought I saw something, but it's so dark..."

"I saw her," Charlotte said, standing by the gate.

Ruth turned to her. "You did?"

Charlotte nodded.

"See?" Ruth continued, turning to her husband. "I wasn't imagining it!"

"I didn't say you *were*," Tony replied. "I saw her too, or at least I thought I did. I just..." He glanced over at Charlotte, and it was clear that he had no idea what to think.

"I saw her," Charlotte said, her heart racing as she walked over to join Ruth. "It wasn't a trick of the light or any of that bullshit. I fucking saw her." She believed it, too. She was even convinced that she'd seen the little girl walking forward. She knew full well that it was possible for shadows to conspire and create an illusion, but that's not what had happened. She *knew* that she'd seen the silhouette of a little girl down by the fence, and yet now there was no sign of her. It was as if she'd briefly shown herself, only to vanish back into the mist.

"Sophie!" Ruth screamed. "Sophie! Where are you?"

"Sophie!" Charlotte shouted.

"You saw her, didn't you?" Ruth said, tears rolling down her face as she turned to her sister. "Please, God, tell me you saw her. Tell me I'm not imagining it!"

"I saw her," Charlotte replied. "I did."

"Are you sure?" Ruth shouted, grabbing her by the arms. "Are you absolutely sure?"

"Of course I'm fucking sure!" Charlotte shouted back at her. "Do you think I'd fucking say anything if I wasn't sure? I saw her! I saw..." She paused for a moment. "I mean, it sure as hell looked like her. I saw her silhouette. I swear to God, I saw her!"

"Sophie!" Tony shouted, trudging through the mud as he made his way toward the tow-path. "Sophie!"

"Where is she?" Ruth asked, turning and following him. "I don't understand. She must have seen us, so why didn't she come to the house? What's wrong with her? Is she scared? Doesn't she remember us?"

Turning to glance back at the house, Charlotte suddenly realized that she could see a figure lumbering toward them through the mist. For a fraction of a second, her heart leaped in her chest as she allowed herself to believe that it might be Sophie, before she realized with crushing horror that it was a different shape altogether. It was someone older, someone less steady, someone who could barely stay upright.

"Fuck," she muttered, hurrying back through the mist until she reached her mother. "Mum, what are you doing? I told you to stay back there!"

"Where is she?" her mother asked, leaning heavily on Charlotte. "I saw her! Where is she?"

"Fuck," Charlotte gasped, straining to keep them both upright. "Mum, you're too heavy." She looked over toward the tow-path. "Hey! Someone! A little help here?"

In the distance, she heard Ruth and Tony calling Sophie's name.

"I guess they're busy," Charlotte muttered as she tried to shift her mother's weight. "Mum, you need to try to straighten your legs," she gasped, feeling as if she was fighting a losing battle to keep them both up. "Seriously, Mum, you need to help me to help you here -"

"Where is she?" the old woman whispered, trying to push on toward the river.

"Let them look," Charlotte continued. "Mum, it's muddy out here -"

"I saw her," her mother insisted. "I saw Charlotte."

"Sophie," Charlotte replied. "You saw Sophie, Mum. And we all saw her." She turned and looked at the darkness all around them, and a chill ran up her spine. "We all did," she continued. "We all saw her."

"It's my fault," her mother said, trying to push her away. "Let me go and find her."

"It's not your fault," Charlotte said, as she heard Ruth and Tony still calling for their daughter, their voices sounding further and further away. "Mum, you're gonna fucking freeze out here. I can't let you down onto the ground. It's muddy as hell."

"It's my fault," her mother continued, still trying to get past until, finally, she tumbled into the fence.

"Here," Charlotte said, wrapping her mother's arms over the top of the gate-post. "Don't let go, okay?"

"Poor Charlotte," her mother said, her milky white eyes fixed on the darkness ahead. "That poor little girl."

"Yeah," Charlotte replied after a moment, finally taking a few seconds to catch her breath. "Poor Charlotte. Poor little girl, huh?" She paused as she listened to the others' voices, still plaintively calling for Sophie in the distance. "We all saw Sophie," she continued after a moment, "and then..." She turned and looked back across the misty lawn. For the first time since all of this had begun, she was starting to reconsider her beliefs. She knew she'd seen the girl's silhouette, and yet it was clear that there was no sign of her. Suddenly, the most rational explanation, the *only* rational explanation, was one that filled Charlotte with fear.

"It's all my fault," her mother whispered, still clinging to the fence. "All of it. The cold. The mud. Everything. I should never... Poor Charlotte."

"It's Sophie, mother," Charlotte replied, starting to get annoyed. "For fuck's sake, can't you pull yourself together for once?" She immediately realized that she was being too harsh, however, and to compensate, she took off her jacket and wrapped it around her mother's shoulders. "It's going to be okay," she said, trying to calm the old woman a little. "It's going to be okay, there's -"

Before she could finish, she spotted the silhouette of a girl nearby, on the grass. For a moment, her heart seemed to stop beating until she realized that the silhouette was actually her own shadow, cast alongside her mother's across the lawn. Still, as she looked more closely, she realized that while her mother's shadow was heaving with the old woman's attempts to stay upright, her own shadow seemed to be completely still and calm, almost as if it was staring back at her, almost as if...

"Ettolrahc," Charlotte whispered.

"It's my fault," her mother continued. "It's my fault that poor Charlotte's dead."

"I'm not dead, Mum," she replied, feeling a cold shiver pass through her body. "It just feels like that sometimes."

In the distance, Ruth and Tony were still calling for their daughter, their unanswered calls drifting through the trees and mist. All Charlotte could do, however, was wait with her mother and hope that somehow the little girl might yet be found, even though - with every distant call of her name - it was now clear that Sophie had disappeared again.

Today

"Where is she?" Charlotte asked, sitting at the kitchen table as Tony came through from the hallway. "Is she okay?"

It was a little after 8am, and while she'd managed to get a couple of hours' sleep, Charlotte was feeling wide awake and deathly tired at the same time, as if she was being pulled in two directions. She was having coffee for breakfast, and she'd decided that she didn't give a damn about actual food. Besides, she'd been feeling nauseous since she woke up, and she was worried she might vomit at any moment.

"Not smoking?" Tony asked as he put the kettle on.

"I quit," she replied.

"No more smoking and no more drinking?" he replied. "Who are you, and what have you done with the real Charlotte?"

"You didn't answer my question," she pointed out, preferring to dodge a few questions herself. "How's Ruth?"

"Resting," he replied. "Tea?"

"Sleeping?"

"Resting." He grabbed a cup and a teabag. "She's very tired after last night. Physically and emotionally. She..." He paused. "It seemed very certain at one point that Sophie was..." He paused again. "You saw her, didn't you? I mean, I know it was dark, but you saw her too!"

Charlotte nodded.

"So what the hell happened?" he continued.

"I don't know," Charlotte replied. She'd been trying to figure things out all morning, but nothing quite made sense. If she was honest, she was starting to wonder whether maybe she was losing her mind. That whole business with Ettolrahc seemed so long ago; according to her mother, she'd spent most of her childhood wrapped up in the fantasy of having some kind of invisible, imaginary best friend who lived inside her body. While she thought it was kind of cute that she'd maybe seen that best friend again last night, she also recognized that in terms of mental health, such a development was hardly ideal.

"I guess there's always next year," Tony muttered, as the kettle finished boiling.

"Next year?"

No reply.

"You can't be serious," she continued, realizing that far from coming to an end, the madness looked set to go on and on. "Tony, you have to stop this. Move on! You can't spend every year waiting for a lost little girl to come back." She waited for a reply, but he was being conspicuously attentive toward his tea, obviously trying to avoid the conversation. "What happened to me," Charlotte added finally, "was a fucking miracle, okay? It was never explained, and it'll probably *never* be explained." Above, there was the sound of movement in her mother's bedroom. "Great," she muttered. "All we need." She took a deep breath, and as she watched Tony fish his teabag from the cup, she realized that she had to say the one thing that she'd been holding back. "Tony?"

"What?"

She paused again, reluctant to say the words but convinced that it was the only option. "Sophie's dead."

"You don't know that."

"I do."

"You don't."

"I *do*!" She paused, filled with desperation as she tried to think of a way to get through to him. "I don't know how, or why, or when, or who did it or even whether anyone did it or if we're ever going to get all the answers, but you have to face the facts." She waited for a reply. "She's obviously dead, Tony. She's not coming back. I *hope* that one day we find out what happened to her, but in the meantime, you and Ruth have to get on with your lives."

"Then what was that thing last night?" he asked, turning to her. "If that wasn't Sophie, who was it?"

"An illusion," she replied, although she felt as if she was on less steady ground. "Sophie's not going to come back."

"*You* did."

"Barely." She paused. "Sometimes I feel as though only half of me came back. Less even. I know that's a shitty thing to say, and it's kinda melodramatic, but it's true." Instinctively, she raised a hand to her mouth, momentarily forgetting that she'd stopped smoking. "God," she muttered, "I need a fag."

"I'm sure you could have one," Tony replied. "Just this once."

She shook her head.

"Why the clean slate?" he asked. "I thought you were going to smoke and drink your way through life?"

"I decided to try another route," she said, finishing her coffee before getting to her feet and wandering over to the back door. "I try not to swear and curse so much, too. Hell, I think I might even give up coffee." She paused, looking out across the still-misty lawn. "Really go for that detox shit, you know? For the future."

"That's the same reason we're not going to give up hope," he replied. "Whatever happens, I still believe that some day, somehow, Sophie's going to come back to us." He paused, and it was clear that although he was struggling to maintain his optimism, he was just about getting by thanks to a combination of desperation and fear. "And there's nothing you can say, Charlotte, that'll ever change my mind, or Ruth's. We just know it in our hearts. Perhaps it's not something you can understand if you're not a parent yourself, but Sophie's coming back. It's just a question of when."

***

A few minutes later, having made a polite excuse to get away from Tony, Charlotte found herself wandering across the lawn, making her way through the strands of mist that lingered from the night before. She didn't really know why she wanted to be outside, except that she was scared she might give in to her nicotine craving if she stayed in the house. Besides, she felt as if the entire house had been draped in a veil of sorrow, and at that particular moment, she wasn't sure whether she ever wanted to go back inside.

Making her way past the fence at the bottom of the garden, she couldn't help but glance over her shoulder, just in case there might be anyone around. The sight of her unmoving shadow the previous night had left a deep impression, and she was reliving all the stories her mother had previously told her about her childhood. Charlotte had never been able to remember much about her life before the day she disappeared, although thanks to tales told by her mother and sister she'd begun to piece things together, and she was well aware of the basic details surrounding her imaginary best friend. She found the idea of Ettolrahc amusing, although the thought that she might start *seeing* things after all these years was mildly disturbing. Still, she figured she at least had something to talk about next time she went to visit Dr. Gould.

When she got to the tow-path and looked down into the river, she found herself trying to remember specific events from her childhood. There were leaves floating on the water now, the first stirrings of autumn, and each leaf seemed like a lost memory, destined to be carried away forever. Her oldest memory, or at least her oldest clear memory, was of the moment she wandered along the tow-path once she'd returned from her year's absence. Everything before her disappearance was somewhat vague and distorted, despite her mother's attempts to help her clarify things by telling her stories and making gentle attempts to nudge her in the right direction. Even after her sessions with Dr. Gould, she'd been unable to dig to far back into her past. It was as if her life before the disappearance was a darkened space from which no memories could escape, and into which she was forbidden from venturing. If her life was a river, it was one that started suddenly, almost as if it came out of nowhere.

After a few minutes, she decided to make her way along the tow-path, toward the cave. She was starting to feel as if this might be the very last time she ever came to the house, at least for a while. It was clear that Ruth and Tony were now locked into their own private pattern of grief, with no immediate indication that they had the will or the ability to get free. If they persisted in waiting for Sophie to come back, there was clearly no chance that they'd be able to live normal lives. Charlotte desperately wanted them to move on, to have another child, but the specter of Sophie seemed set to haunt them for many years to come. Matters weren't helped, of course, by the bizarre sight that had greeted them all last night, when -

As she reached the approach to the cave, Charlotte suddenly stopped dead in her tracks.

It couldn't be...

She stared into the water, gripped by the most terrible fear. She wanted to believe that her eyes were deceiving her, that somehow she was imagining the whole thing, but deep down she knew that it was so horribly real. More and more leaves were slowly drifting past, borne on the current that kept the river moving, but among those leaves there was something else, something larger, something spread out in the shape of a star, with leaves on its back as it drifted face-down along the surface of the water, slowly bumping into the edge of the river before beginning the slow, lifeless drift back out into the current, parting the carpet of leaves as she went.

A dead girl. Young, her arms and legs outstretched. She looked so peaceful, and so natural, that Charlotte didn't scream at all. She simply took a step back, with tears in her eyes, and she realized with terrible finality that Sophie had finally come back after all.

Today

"A pound for a bag of crisps?" Charlotte said, staring dry-eyed at the vending machine's prices. "Are you fucking kidding me? A pound?"

She took a step back, before glancing along the corridor and realizing that there was no-one nearby to hear her protest. Sighing, she searched through her pocket for some coins, before slipping two fifty pences into the slot and pressing the green button. Slowly, the bag of crisps was pushed forward before dropping down into the slot, and Charlotte fished them out, opened them, and took a bite.

"Tastes like shit," she muttered.

It was getting late, and she was in a corridor at the local police station. She was trying to fill her mind with dull, awkward thoughts, in the hope that she could prevent herself from thinking about anything more difficult. So far, by focusing on the vending machine and other banal objects, she'd managed to almost completely avoid contemplating the reason for her visit, although occasional distant voices were a reminder that elsewhere in the building, the job of 'processing' Sophie's body was well underway.

"Can I help you?" asked a voice nearby.

Turning, Charlotte saw a young female police officer waiting by a nearby door.

"Sorry?" Charlotte asked.

"Are you here to see someone?"

"I'm just pissed off about this vending machine," she replied. "I mean, I could get these same crisps for half the price in town, so why am I being ripped off? People are vulnerable in a place like this, so it seems kinda unfair to rip them off when they're hardly in a state to be dealing with this kind of shit."

The officer stared at her.

"And another thing," Charlotte continued, "why don't you offer free food and drinks for people, huh? You'd think it'd be a nice thing to do, wouldn't it? Just fucking... give a little, you know? Hell, if I ran the police, I'd give out a free shot of whiskey to anyone who's had a bad time. I really think you need to rethink how you deal with people who've... who've been traumatized, you know? People who've had really fucking bad days."

They stood in silence for a moment.

"So can I help you in any way?" the officer asked eventually.

"I'm fine," Charlotte replied, turning and hurrying off in the opposite direction. The last thing she wanted was to get dragged into a conversation with some random woman, so she made her way quickly around the next corner, finally coming face to face with Tony, who was slouched in a chair in the small waiting room. While Charlotte had been spending her time trying to burn off all her excess energy, and trying to forget the image of the girl's body floating along the river, Tony seemed to have gone the opposite way: he'd fallen completely still, as if he was off in some other, inner world.

"Hey," he said flatly.

"Crisp?" Charlotte asked, holding the bag out to him.

He shook his head.

"They're pretty rank," Charlotte continued, looking down into the bag. "I don't even know why I'm eating them, really. I guess it's 'cause I paid a pound for them. A whole fucking pound. I mean, can you believe that? People don't come to police stations for fun. They come because something bad has happened, and then they're fucking gouged for a pound just 'cause they want to eat a packet of crisps. Can you believe the fucking... cruelty and hypocrisy of the whole thing?"

Tony stared at her.

"You know what I mean," she muttered.

"Ruth's talking to someone," Tony said after a moment. "They're still trying to work out Sophie's movements before she ended up in the river, and for some reason, they want to talk to us separately." He paused, his face completely devoid of emotion. "I guess they want to make sure that we give honest answers, rather than getting our stories all mixed up together. Makes sense, if you think about it. They should -" He paused, with tears in his eyes, and it was as if suddenly he'd seized up completely.

"Have they..." Charlotte paused. "I mean, have they formally identified the..."

They stood in silence for a moment.

"Sorry," she added.

"Not yet," Tony replied, "but, I mean, there's no..." His voice tailed off. "It's not like there were any other eight-year-old girls missing in that area," he added finally, "so I think it's safe to..." He took a deep breath, before looking down at his hands. "I know it's stupid," he continued after a moment, "and I know I really had no reason to think it, but I swear to God, I was convinced she was going to come back to us. Right up until the end, I was certain this would all be okay." There were tears in his eyes again, and his voice was cracking. "Deep down in my heart, I was absolutely sure that she'd..."

Charlotte watched as he broke down into a fit of sobs. After a moment, she took another crisp from the packet and gave it a nibble. She felt hopelessly useless around people who were exhibiting real emotions. Her usual tactics - sarcasm, humor and, at a push, escape - seemed inappropriate, and she didn't feel that she had anything else to offer.

"She was such a good girl," Tony continued eventually. "She was so smart and energetic and creative. I know every parent thinks that about their child, but with Sophie, it was really true. Even her teachers said so."

Charlotte opened her mouth to say something, but no words came out. She just kept replaying those final moments over and over again, when she'd been teasing Sophie.

"Do you know the weird part?" Tony asked. "I'd actually started to believe that she might come back the same way *you* came back. I thought she'd stay away for a year and then come wandering back to the house. It sounds ridiculous now, but somehow it started to make sense. I didn't even care how it was going to happen. I just figured... somehow, she was going to return. I told myself to be cautious and not to expect too much, but at the same time, I couldn't stop believing. It all feels so stupid now."

"It's not stupid," Charlotte replied, trying to fight the nausea she was starting to feel. "I was the same."

"Really?"

She nodded. "And Ruth -"

"Ruth has been frantic over the past year," he continued. "She used to go out for long walks every day. She pretended she was just getting some air, but I knew the real reason. She was looking for her. She probably scoured every inch of the countryside around our house, terrified that any moment she might uncover..." He paused for a moment. "And all along she was so close to the house. I guess she must have been wedged somewhere, and eventually she came loose. I still don't get why the divers didn't find her, though. They said they looked everywhere."

"There's no point blaming anyone," Charlotte pointed out, hearing footsteps nearby. Glancing along the corridor, she saw a couple of police officers heading through a set of double doors. One of them was Eve, the officer she remembered from the previous year, and she had a stern, worried look on her face.

"I don't know if I can face this," Tony said quietly.

"It's okay," Charlotte said, putting an arm around his shoulders.

"Hi," Eve said as she and the other officers reached them. There was a clear sense of nervousness in her voice, as if she was reluctant to deliver whatever news she was supposed to bring. "We've completed the identification procedure regarding the body," she continued uncertainly. "We... had to go back into some of the old files, some of the records from quite a while ago, but I'm afraid we now have a formal, confirmed identification. It's been signed off by the coroner, and the details have now been entered into the official record."

"It's okay," Tony said, his voice sounding weak and forlorn. "I know there's -"

"It's not Sophie," Eve said suddenly.

Charlotte stared at her, while Tony seemed not to have heard. It was as if time had stood still for a moment, as if the whole of the universe had suddenly swiveled and begun to pivot on that cool, flickering corridor.

"What?" Charlotte said eventually.

"It's not Sophie," Eve continued, but she didn't seem relieved. "Absolutely, one hundred per cent, we are positive that it's not Sophie." She paused. "We've... Actually, we've completed the identification procedure, and we know whose body it is."

Charlotte and Tony exchanged a stunned glance, before both turning to Eve.

"Who is it?" Charlotte asked, her heart pounding in her chest.

"It's..." Eve stared at her for a moment, as if she could barely bring herself to say the words. "It's you, Charlotte," she continued eventually. "The body we pulled from the river is you. It's Charlotte Abernathy."

Part Four

Rising

Twenty years ago

She walked forward on weak, uncertain legs, unsure of her destination. Every step felt heavy and forced, and as she made her way along the uneven tow-path, she tried to focus on the simple act of making her way to the gap in the trees. Just as she'd been told, just as she remembered, there was a small fence and an open wooden gate.

    Leaning against the fence, she looked across the wide open lawn, at the house that stood alone in the distance. Just a couple of hundred meters to go, but it felt like all the distance in the world. Still, she knew that she couldn't stop, not yet. She had to keep going, because otherwise she'd just end up dying where she stood. Blood was trickling down her leg, and she was having trouble breathing. As she stared at the house, she felt a wave of dizziness wash over her, and she had to cling to the wooden fence-post for a moment longer before finally she was able to regain her balance. Taking as deep a breath as she could manage, she realized that it was now or never.

    She tried to run, but all she could really do was stumble as fast as possible across the sloping lawn, making her way quickly toward the house. She felt desperately light-headed, and every few steps she found herself swaying a little, which forced her to focus on righting herself before she tumbled down onto the grass. At one point, about halfway, she lost her footing entirely and had to halt her fall by reaching out with her hands, pushing herself back up and continuing her journey. The back door of the house was open, so she knew that someone had to be at home. She just needed to take a few more painful, tottering steps.

When she reached the door, she stopped for a moment, trying to get her head to stop spinning. She could see a woman in the kitchen, working at the stove, and a young girl at the nearby table. For a moment, she just stared at them, until suddenly the young girl glanced at her and stared in shocked silence. A few seconds later, the woman looked over, and there was a brief moment of absolute silence. The whole universe stopped for a moment.

Today

"You don't have to do this," Eve said. "I think it might be -"

"Let me see," Charlotte said firmly. She wasn't crying and she wasn't angry. She just wanted to see it with her own eyes.

They were standing in a room at the back of the station. In the center of the room there was a table, and on the table there was a dead body, covered by a sheet. Nearby, a trolley contained a couple of empty metal pans, along with the various medical instruments that would have been used, earlier, for the autopsy.

"She's not in the best condition," Eve said after a moment. "I should warn you that -"

"Let me see," Charlotte said again, stepping forward this time and pulling the sheet away to reveal the young girl's putrescent face, its rotten skin having been reduced in places to a kind of thick, discolored soup. Her eyes were completely gone, and her mouth was slightly open, exposing a delicate row of gray teeth.

"The cause of death is believed to have been hypothermia," Eve said, "along with blood loss. She had a broken ankle and some other cuts and bruises."

"She?" Charlotte replied, her eyes fixed on the horrific sight.

"Charlotte Abernathy," Eve said calmly.

"I'm Charlotte Abernathy," Charlotte whispered.

"Well," Eve replied, "that's something we have to talk about." She reached out to put the sheet back over the dead girl's face.

"Wait," Charlotte said, pushing the sheet away again. She leaned closer, staring at the hollow, partially-collapsed sockets that once contained the girl's eyes. After a moment, she reached out and, with just a single fingertip, touched the rotten flesh on the side of the corpse's face.

"We should talk somewhere else," Eve said, clearly uncomfortable.

"The bitch," Charlotte replied.

"I'm sorry?"

Charlotte paused. "The bitch," she said again, taking a step back. Her mind was racing and she couldn't get her head around what she was seeing.

"Who are you referring to?" Eve asked.

Charlotte turned to her. "The bitch who did this to me," she said after a moment. "The bitch whose fault this all is."

Twenty years ago

"Charlotte!" the woman shouted, hurrying toward her.

Charlotte held onto the side of the door, still worried about falling.

"Oh Charlotte!" the woman said, kneeling in front of her and staring, as if she couldn't believe what she was seeing. "Charlotte, what... Where have you been? My God, where were you?"

Charlotte opened her mouth to reply, but something seemed wrong. It was as if her thoughts were spinning, and as the woman continued to stare at her, Charlotte tried to understand her place among these people. The truth, though, was that something felt terribly wrong, as if her mother's hands - which even now were pawing at her, holding her tight and checking to make sure that she was solid - were alien and strange.

"Oh my God," the woman said, pulling her close and embracing her with force. "Oh my God, Charlotte, you came home! Where have you been?"

Charlotte stared over the woman's shoulder, watching the little girl at the table, who seemed to be viewing her with suspicion.

"We were so worried about you," the woman continued, letting go of Charlotte and leaning back to get a better view of her. "Are you hurt? Charlotte, who were you with? Did someone take you? What happened? Did someone hurt you? Charlotte, this is very important. Did anyone do things to you?"

Charlotte shook her head.

"What does that mean?" the woman replied, getting to her feet before taking Charlotte's hand and leading her over to the table. "Ruth, look! Your sister has come back! After a whole year, your sister has come back to us! Isn't this the most wonderful day in the whole world?"

Ruth stared at Charlotte, but she didn't seem nearly so pleased to see her.

"Have you been fed?" the woman asked, placing the back of her hand against Charlotte's forehead. "You feel okay, and you look healthy, but where have you been? We've been searching for you, sweetheart. We've looked everywhere! You've been gone for a whole year!" She waited for an answer. "Who were you with, Charlotte?"

Charlotte turned to look up at her. "I..." she started to say, before feeling as if she might faint. She waited a moment, and slowly she was able to steady herself. "I was..."

"Sit down," her mother said, pulling a chair out from the table before steering Charlotte into the seat. "You must be hungry and thirsty," she added, hurrying over to the counter and grabbing the biscuit barrel, before placing it in front of Charlotte.

"Your sister needs this," she said to Ruth as she grabbed her glass of juice and slid it in front of Charlotte. "Eat," she continued. "Drink. Then we'll get you cleaned up, okay?"

Charlotte stared at the biscuit barrel. She didn't much feel like eating anything, but she felt that she had no choice. It was as if the whole world was new and strange, filled with terrifying sensations that echoed in her mind. She knew that she was supposed to find this place and these people familiar, but they shrieked with strangeness and nothing seemed able to settle her thoughts. In her mind's eye, she had images of other people, images that didn't make sense, but she didn't feel equipped to work out what was really happening.

"I'll have to call the police and let them know you're back," the woman said after a moment. "I'm sure they'll want to make a big fuss, but we'll soon get things back to normal. That's all that matters, really, isn't it? Getting things back to normal? Charlotte, sweetheart..." She paused, with tears in her eyes. "Ruth," she said, turning to the other girl, "aren't you so pleased to have you sister back? Isn't this the moment we've been praying and hoping for?"

Slowly, Charlotte turned to the other girl and was met with a firm scowl.

"Wait right here," the woman said, hurrying through to the hallway so she could make a phone call.

Charlotte sat quietly, aware that Ruth seemed to be studying her intently. It was an awkward moment, the silence filled with tension.

"I'm back," Charlotte said tentatively, hoping to make things feel a little more normal.

Ruth stared at her.

"I'm back," Charlotte said again. "I guess."

Silence.

"Huh," Ruth said eventually, narrowing her eyes, almost as if she didn't believe what she was seeing.

Today

"Where is she?" Charlotte shouted, banging the front door open as she stormed into the house. "Where's that fucking bitch?"

"Calm down," Ruth called after her, as she and Tony followed. "This isn't going to solve anything!"

Ignoring her sister, Charlotte bounded up the stairs two-at-a-time, before hurrying to her mother's bedroom and swinging the door open. The old woman was tucked in her bed, on her side, and she didn't respond as Charlotte hurried across the room and grabbed her by the shoulder, forcibly rolling her onto her back.

"What -" Charlotte started to say, but the words became stuck in her throat as she stared down at the old woman's scared, white eyes.

"Leave her alone!" Ruth shouted, barging into the room and taking hold of Charlotte by the arm, trying to pull her away. "Jesus Christ, Charlotte, this isn't how you're supposed to do it!"

"I want to know what she did," Charlotte continued, pulling free of her sister's grip. Staring down at her mother, she saw nothing but weakness and fear, but at the same time she was filled with more anger than she'd ever felt in her life. "Tell me," she continued, her voice trembling as she knelt by the bed. "Tell me what the fuck you did twenty years ago."

Her bottom lip wobbling, the old woman stared at Charlotte, as if she had no idea what she was talking about, or even who she was.

"She's having one of her bad days," Ruth continued breathlessly. "She doesn't remember anything, Charlotte. There's no point trying to force it. All you're doing is torturing a scared old woman."

"Good," Charlotte said, keeping her eyes fixed on her mother. "I think right now I'd quite like to torture her."

"Can we talk about this downstairs?" Ruth asked.

"And let her just go back to sleep?" Charlotte replied, before leaning closer to her mother's face. "It's time to come clean, you old bitch," she continued, her voice trembling with rage. "I don't care if you're demented. I don't care if your fucking mind is falling apart at the seams, but you're going to come around right now, you're going to find one moment of fucking lucidity, and you're gonna tell me what the fuck you did to me!"

"Who are you?" her mother whispered, trying to curl up into the far corner of the bed.

"That's what *I* want to know!" Charlotte sneered, grabbing her shoulder and forcing her onto her back.

"Help!" the old woman shrieked. "Somebody help me!"

"That's enough!" Ruth said, grabbing Charlotte and pulling her away with such force that she ended up slamming her sister into the wardrobe. "You're not going to get anything from her!" she continued. "Look at her! She's lost her mind, Charlotte. Even if she wanted to tell you every detail of her life, she doesn't even know who any of us are!" She paused. "You haven't been here over the past year. You haven't seen how badly she's deteriorated. She comes out of this daze about once a week, at most. The rest of the time, she floats along. You want to know the most we can hope for on an average day? That she doesn't soil herself!"

"She's not getting away with it that easily," Charlotte replied, her eyes still fixed on her mother's terrified form and her eyes still filled with tears and venom. "I'll sit right here all day and all night until she's ready to talk."

"It won't do any good," Ruth replied. "Please, come downstairs and we'll talk. Maybe we can figure this out."

Charlotte stared at her mother for a moment longer.

"Charlotte?" Ruth continued. "Will you come downstairs with me?"

"Maybe," Charlotte whispered. "Fine. Yes."

"Come on," Ruth said, reaching out a hand to help her up. "I'm sure we can muddle through."

Slowly, achingly, Charlotte got to her feet, placing one hand on her belly to make sure she was okay. She took a couple of steps toward the door, before finally realizing that there was no way she could back out so easily. Turning back to the bed, she sat on the edge and leaned over her mother once more, ready to scream in her face.

"I'm sorry," her mother said, her eyes wide with terror.

"About what?" Charlotte asked.

"For God's sake," Ruth muttered, trying to pull Charlotte away.

"I shouldn't have done it," the old woman continued. "I'm so sorry. I should have just let the truth be the truth."

"Leave her alone," Ruth continued.

"No," Charlotte said, pushing her away. "I think she knows what she's saying."

"I loved that girl so much," her mother continued, with tears in her eyes. "She was trouble, especially after her father died, but she had more heart than her sister. More passion. Ruth was always so obedient and well-behaved. Easier to deal with, but not nearly so rewarding. Charles and I both thought that Charlotte had more to offer, more potential. After Charles died, I had to struggle on as best I could, but I always knew that Charlotte was the one who... Charlotte was always going to be the special one. So much smarter and brighter and more vital than her sister."

"Fuck you," Ruth muttered under her breath, standing by the door.

"Go on," Charlotte said, her eyes fixed on her mother.

"When Charlotte disappeared," the old woman continued, "I was heartbroken. I'd tried so hard to tame that poor young girl, to keep her safe without dulling her, but I couldn't contain her energy. She had such a wild imagination. She used to talk about imaginary friends, and witches, and all sorts of things. And then one day, she was just... gone. The police looked everywhere, but eventually they scaled back their search. I begged them to continue, but they said they'd done all they could. They kept the case open, of course, and they promised to keep working on it, but I knew there was nothing more they could do. So I just had to wait and hope that my special little girl would somehow find her way back to me. It didn't seem impossible, but as the months went past, and there was no sign of Charlotte..."

Charlotte and Ruth waited a moment, each of them trapped in their own private moment of shock.

"One day," their mother continued, "quite by chance, I was in Farnborough, of all places. I was alone. I'd left Ruth at home by herself. She seemed old enough. I was at the market, and I saw this awful, awful woman pushing her child around. Such cruelty and meanness. I wondered how such a terrible person could ever raise a little girl, and then when the girl looked at me, I saw fear and sorrow in her eyes. I followed them through the crowd, and then I saw the little girl wander off, as if she was trying to get away from her mother. I went after her, and I know I should have just taken her back to where she belonged, but instead... I wanted to cheer her up, so I took her for ice cream. She was the same age as Charlotte, and she looked a little like her. It wasn't hard to convince myself that..." Her voice trailed off for a moment, as tears trickled down her face.

"Jesus Christ," Ruth muttered, wiping tears from her eyes.

"She had bruises on her arms," the old woman continued. "She wanted to get away. She was a few years younger than Charlotte, but nothing that couldn't be fudged."

"This girl you found at the market," Charlotte said, dry-eyed and calm. "She..."

They sat in silence for a moment.

"I brought her home," the old woman whispered. "I should never have done such a thing, but I did. By the time we got to the house, I knew I'd made a mistake, but it was too late, so I made her stay all alone in the old shed that Charles used to use for his gardening. I kept her in there for a few months. I told her to be quiet, and I trained her, slowly. I knew it would never work, but gradually I was able to convince her that her old life had been a dream. I started calling her Charlotte, and to my wonder, she seemed to take the name on quite happily. She was still young and impressionable. It shouldn't have worked, but it did, and I started to think that God had delivered this miracle to me. It must have been a miracle, mustn't it? That's the only possible explanation. It's the only thing that makes sense. Finally, once I was sure that she had begun to believe all the lies I told her, I realized that I needed to work out how to bring her into the family."

"This is insane," Charlotte replied. "You can't just wipe a young girl's mind like that and put new memories into her head."

"You don't understand," her mother said quietly. "That little girl didn't *want* to go back to her wicked mother. She let me fill her head with all these new ideas. It was like an unspoken understanding between us. Maybe she thought it was a game at first, but eventually it all took root. I was constantly surprised by how easy the whole thing seemed to be, but what was I supposed to do? I decided to wait a few more weeks, until the anniversary of her disappearance, and..." She paused. "It still shouldn't have worked, but I suppose people want to believe a miracle, and perhaps I was a little lucky in places, and it's not as if we have a big family. So it simply became accepted that this young girl *was* Charlotte. I never stopped thinking about the real Charlotte, of course, but I gradually taught the new girl more and more about her old life, and soon I realized it was too late to stop. I thought it would come crashing down one day, so I just waited, and everything began to become normal again."

"I was that girl," Charlotte whispered, looking over at the window. "My name's not Charlotte at all." She paused, before turning back to her mother. "What was my real name?"

"I never knew," the old woman replied, with tears still trickling down her face. "I never asked."

"The real Charlotte never came back," Charlotte replied. "The police think her body was trapped in the cave for all these years and then somehow, finally, it came loose and began to drift along the river. She was dead all along."

"My poor little girl," her mother whispered, her voice filled with tears. "My poor little Charlotte. She must have been so scared and alone in her final moments. So cold. If only I'd been able to find her. If only the police had done a better job of looking. She must have suffered terribly. That was always the part that worried me the most." Filled with sobs, she stared up at the ceiling, her eyes overflowing with tears. "I should have kept her safe."

Charlotte sat in silence for a moment, overwhelmed by the realization that her entire life had been a lie. She tried to think back to the moment when she'd first wandered along the tow-path, back past that first memory to the life she'd lived before, but it was no use. Her memories seemed to be blocked, and she could only assume that in some way, she'd been complicit in the decision all those years ago to hide her former life. It was too much to take in, and all she could do was wait for the chaos to be over.

"I'm so sorry," her mother whispered. "I'm such a terrible person. Poor Sophie."

"Sophie?" Charlotte replied with tears in her eyes. "Poor *Sophie*? What about *me*? What about Charlotte? What about -" She paused for a moment, staring at her mother's frail, aged face, and finally she realized that there was no point directing her fury at this pathetic old woman. The whole thing just felt completely futile. "What about Ruth? What about everyone?"

"I'm so sorry," her mother said, her voice so quiet now that she could barely be heard. "Poor Sophie."

"What *about* Sophie?" Charlotte asked eventually, looking over at Ruth. "Where is she?"

"I -" Ruth started to say, but the words seemed to be sticking in her throat.

"Ruth?" Charlotte continued, with a slow sense of realization starting to creep up through her body. "Where's Sophie?"

"You wouldn't understand," Ruth replied. "Leave it be."

"Where is she?" Charlotte asked again, more firmly this time.

Ruth paused for a moment. "I think..." She paused again. "I think you'd better come with me," she said eventually. "I suppose... I've got something to show you."

Twenty years ago

"It's okay, Charlotte," the police officer said, smiling as she leaned closer. "I just want to get an idea of where you've been for the past year. Is that okay? Do you want to talk to me?"

Charlotte stared at the woman for a moment, before glancing over at her mother, who responded with a brief nod. Turning back to the police officer, Charlotte narrowed her eyes as she stared at the woman's face. "Okay," she said eventually, even though she would have preferred to have gone upstairs to play alone in her room. Still, her mother had promised her that the police officer's visit would be over soon, so she figured she should just be polite.

"You were gone for a very long time," the officer continued. "Do you realize that? Your mother and your sister were very worried about you. Everyone was worried. We had people out looking for you. We even had divers in the river, in case you'd got into trouble while you were swimming."

Charlotte waited for a question. So far, she felt that people were just talking to her, telling her things that she should already know.

"So can you tell me where you were?" the officer asked. "I know it might be difficult, but everyone here wants to help you. It's just that when little girls go missing, even if they come back and everything seems okay, we like to make sure that they were okay while they were gone. Do you understand that?"

Charlotte paused. "I don't know," she said eventually.

"You don't know where you were?"

Charlotte shook her head.

The police officer looked over at Charlotte's mother, before turning back to Charlotte. "It's okay," she said after a moment. "You're not in any trouble. No-one thinks you've been naughty."

"I know I'm not in trouble," Charlotte replied. "I just don't know where I was." She took a deep breath, aware that both the police officer and her mother were staring at her. She felt as if no-one believed her, even though she was doing her best to answer their questions.

"What's the last thing you remember before today?"

"I..." Charlotte paused again. "I don't know."

"Do you remember being with anyone?"

She shook her head.

"You must have missed your family, though. Do you remember missing them?"

She looked over at her mother.

"It's okay," her mother said calmly. "Be honest."

Turning back to face the police officer, Charlotte paused for a moment. "No," she said finally.

"Do you remember anything at all? Even the slightest thing? We just need one memory, somewhere to start."

"I remember walking along the tow-path this morning," Charlotte replied. She was trying to think back to an earlier moment, back to the time before today, but her memory was hazy. A few vague images and impressions loomed from the darkness, but nothing she could wrangle into clarity. It was as if a lock had been placed on her earlier memories, and although she tried to push her way past -

"Perhaps Charlotte is tired," her mother said suddenly, breaking her train of thought. "She's had such a hard day."

"I appreciate that," said the officer, "but I think -"

"She doesn't remember," Charlotte's mother continued, crossing the room and putting a hand on Charlotte's shoulder as if, suddenly, she was taking charge of the situation. "Maybe she never will. We can try to push her, but I imagine that a child's mind is harder to unravel."

"But still -"

"I'll talk to her," her mother said firmly. "If she's going to open up to anyone, it'll be me."

The officer was clearly a little concerned, glancing first at Charlotte and then back at her mother.

"I really must stress the importance of having a trained professional talk to her," the officer said after a moment. "The sooner we get started, the more likely we are to be able to get to the truth."

"Let me tell you something about my daughter," Charlotte's mother replied. "I know her. She's a delicate and sensitive young girl, and I can assure you, she won't respond well to having some stranger try to burrow her way into her mind. It's better if I'm left to talk to her. If anything's to come out, it'll be when she's talking to me, not to anyone else." She paused. "Do you intend to force the matter and add to her suffering?"

The officer paused. "I can't make you put Charlotte into therapy," she said after a moment, clearly choosing her words carefully, "but I really wish you'd reconsider. A trained psychiatrist has techniques that -"

"A psychiatrist's training is no match for a mother's instinct," came the reply. "I'm her mother, and I know her best." With that, she gave Charlotte's shoulder a reassuring squeeze.

"But -"

"I think we're done here," Charlotte's mother added, as if to end the conversation. "There's no good that can possibly come from talking about this any further. We'll only end up disturbing the girl, and I feel that her future happiness and contentment are more important than delving into the past. You've already had her physically examined and determined that nothing untoward happened in that regard. It seems to me that there's no likelihood of some marauding monster being out there in the wilderness, preying on young girls, and I won't have my daughter's fragile psyche disturbed simply to satisfy your professional curiosity."

"You seem to have made your decision," the officer replied, starting to pack her notes away. "I think you're making a mistake, but -"

"She's back," Charlotte's mother pointed out, leaning down and giving Charlotte a hug. "That's all the matters. I thought she was lost forever, but she came back. She seems to be okay, and that's the most important thing." She paused. "Charlotte, why don't you go upstairs and play with Ruth for a few minutes while I talk to the nice police officer?"

Charlotte paused, feeling as if something was wrong. For a moment, she felt a memory trying to push through her mind; something about a market, and a woman scolding her for losing her gloves, and then she had an image of another woman leading her away, as if -

"Charlotte," her mother said, a little more firmly this time, "I'd like you to go upstairs."

Without replying, Charlotte turned and headed through to the hallway. She could hear her mother still talking to the police officer as they went to the front door, and as she made her way up the stairs, Charlotte couldn't help but think that something still felt very wrong. She knew she should be pleased to be back home, and she felt as if she was being ungrateful, but the whole house seemed strangely unfamiliar, and she had no sense that she'd ever really met her mother or her sister before. Sitting on the top step, she listened to the distant voice of her mother as the police officer was herded out of the house. Finally, the front door slammed shut, and Charlotte realized that she was alone with these people. With a deep breath, she decided that the problem was entirely her fault, and that she'd just have to work hard to fit in with the rest of her family.

She felt certain that she'd feel normal again one day, even if it took a little longer than expected.

Today

"You knew," Charlotte said as she followed Ruth across the lawn, heading to the bottom of the garden. "You knew about it all, didn't you?"

Ahead of her, Ruth said nothing. She just kept walking, leading her sister past the rundown old greenhouse and toward the tow-path.

"Admit it," Charlotte said, her mind still racing as she tried to make sense of everything. She felt that she was on the verge of tears, except something was forcing her to stay strangely, preternaturally calm. "You knew. All this time, you knew and you never said anything."

"I *suspected*," Ruth replied as they reached the tow-path and started walking along the side of the river. "I didn't know, but I suspected. There's a difference." She led Charlotte toward the cave, but finally they headed off through the forest until they came to the little shed that their father had used all those years ago. As she reached the door, Ruth stopped to get the keys from her pocket. "When you came back," she continued, "I knew that something was wrong. I looked at you, and I felt... It wasn't you. Everyone else accepted you so easily, but I could tell it wasn't really you. As I grew up, I became more and more convinced that the real Charlotte had never come back, that you were some kind of imposter, but I couldn't work out why. It wasn't until much later that it even occurred to me that our dear saint of a mother might actually be involved."

Charlotte watched as, with trembling hands, Ruth unfastened the padlock and swung the door open. Seconds later, a young girl came running out of the shed and clasped her arms around Ruth's waist, hugging her tightly. After a year's absence, Sophie was finally back.

"You kept her in here?" Charlotte asked, stunned by the thought that her own sister could be so cruel. "You kidnapped your own daughter?"

"Hey, sweetheart," Ruth said as she crouched in front of Sophie and gave her a kiss on the cheek. "Look, I brought your auntie Charlotte to see you."

Running over, Sophie gave Charlotte a hug.

"I missed you!" the little girl said, although she seemed happy enough. After a moment, she turned back to Ruth. "Does this mean we can go home now?" she asked. "I miss my bedroom!"

Ruth nodded.

"I want to see Daddy," Sophie said.

"Go on," Ruth replied. "Run ahead. Just remember what I told you to say, okay? Daddy's going to be very pleased to see you, you know. Just tell him what we rehearsed, and everything'll be fine."

With a grin, Sophie turned and ran through the forest, making her way back toward the house.

"You kept her in this place?" Charlotte asked, stepping past Charlotte and peering into the shed. It was immediately clear that Ruth had gone to great lengths to ensure that Sophie had been comfortable. There was a bed, and a little table with a lamp, and various toys and games, and even a games console. It was like some kind of perfect hidden den. "You kept your own daughter locked up for a year?" she continued, turning to Ruth. "For a whole year?"

"She was happy down here," Ruth replied cautiously, her voice filled with tension but also a strange kind of pride. "I made sure she had everything she could possibly want. I told Tony I was going for long walks, but in reality I was coming down here to spend time with Sophie. I told her that Tony was busy, and I was able to distract her enough that she didn't push too hard to go back to the house. She had trouble sleeping at night, at least at first, but eventually I was able to make her see that it was fun to be out here. She didn't have to go to school, she didn't have to eat her vegetables or do anything she didn't want to do. I turned it into a game, and she played along. She was very brave."

"But the police must have searched the shed," Charlotte said after a moment. "They went over every inch of this place."

Smiling sadly, Ruth walked over to the far side of the room and reached down, before slowly lifting the edge of a floorboard. "I got Sophie to hide in the same place where Mum made you hide all those years ago, while she was persuading you to forget your old life and teaching you to be Charlotte. The power of suggestion, huh?" She paused. "I told Sophie it was part of the game. She had to be very quiet and very good."

"For a year?" Charlotte asked. "No way. There's no way a kid could -"

"I drugged her," Ruth replied suddenly. "There. Are you happy? It wasn't the plan at first, but after a few days I realized... She slept a lot. A *lot*. I knew I was stepping over a line, but I had no other way." Pausing again, she lowered the loose floorboard. "I had to force the issue, Charlotte. If I hadn't done all of this, we'd have all had to carry on pretending that you came back when we both knew, deep down, that something was wrong."

"But why?" Charlotte asked. "What possessed you to do something like this to your own daughter?"

"I had to make that old bitch tell the truth," Ruth replied, the pride in her voice replaced by a kind of hard, cold anger. "I'd pretty much managed to piece together what had happened, but I needed to force the truth out. At first, I thought that if Sophie disappeared for a few days, it'd force you to remember the truth. When that didn't happen, I realized that I needed to string things out a lot longer and force Mum to..." She paused. "I was willing to push Mum right over the edge, you know. All I cared about was the truth. I was convinced that

Sophie's disappearance would eventually spur her to come clean, but the dementia complicated things. I was starting to think of ways to bring the whole thing to an end, and then..." She paused. "And then my sister's poor little body turned up, like a miracle."

"Did you make that happen too?" Charlotte asked. "Did you find the body?"

Ruth shook her head. "That was a coincidence."

"Hell of a coincidence," Charlotte muttered.

"It *was*, though," Ruth insisted. "It was just a horrific coincidence."

They stood in silence for a moment.

"I don't believe you," Charlotte said eventually.

Ruth shrugged, as if she'd given up trying to defend herself.

"And the little girl's silhouette the other night? Was that your doing as well?"

"No," Ruth replied. "At first, I thought that Sophie had maybe left the shed and come back to the house. I was panicking, but it wasn't Sophie."

"Then who was it?"

Ruth shrugged. "A trick of the light? Shadows? A coincidence, I guess."

"A coincidence that happened right before Charlotte's body just *happened* to break loose and float along the river?" Charlotte replied, trying to work out what, exactly, had happened. She couldn't shake the feeling that there was one final part of the puzzle left to fall into place. After all, it seemed too neat that she'd spotted the body just a few hours after the whole family had seen a girl's silhouette in the darkness.

"What Mum did," Ruth continued after a moment, "was illegal. She deserves to go to jail."

"You're one to talk," Charlotte replied. "Did Tony know about all of this?"

"Not a thing. I kept him completely out of everything."

"How fucking dumb must he be?" Charlotte asked.

"I fed him little morsels of hope," Ruth said. "He's always been very pliable. Sometimes I though he'd begun to suspect everything, but he kept quiet."

"So you let him believe that his daughter was missing?" Charlotte replied. "For a whole year?"

"He'd never have gone along with it."

"Of course he wouldn't. It's insane."

"The truth isn't insane," she replied. "The truth is never a bad thing. Sure, I had to bend a few rules in order to tease it out, but we got there in the end. Sophie's not going to be damaged by all of this. She'll be fine. I made sure to home-school her while she was in the shed." She paused. "I'm certain that you'll understand my point of view eventually," she added after a moment. "When you get past your sense of shock and righteous indignation, you'll realize that this all had to happen."

"You're out of your mind," Charlotte replied. "You crazy bitch, you're stone cold out of your fucking mind."

Ruth smiled. "All I wanted was to force the truth to the surface. Was that so bad? We're the victims in all of this, Charlotte. Mum lied to me and made me believe you were my sister, and she took you away from your real family and forced you to be someone else." She paused. "So are you going to go and tell everyone the truth? Or are you going to accept that everything I did, I did in the name of family, and truth, and love?"

Charlotte stared at her sister for a moment, unable to comprehend the insanity of everything she was hearing. The thought of Sophie being held in the shed for a whole year, regardless of how often Ruth visited and kept her entertained, was shocking, and Charlotte felt as if there was no end to the madness. Still, at the heart of the storm, there was the reality that a young girl had died. Charlotte Abernathy, eight years old, had been killed in a horrible accident in the cave, falling to her death and probably freezing in the darkness.

"What are you going to do?" Ruth asked. "Are you going to report me for what I did?"

"Report you?" Charlotte paused. "I... no."

"You'd have every right to," Ruth continued. "I wasted police time. I abducted my own daughter. I'm sure they'd be very interested to talk to me."

"I'll make sure Tony knows," Charlotte replied. "As long as he gets Sophie away from you, that's enough for me."

"Don't talk nonsense," Ruth replied.

"We'll see."

"And what about Mum?"

Charlotte shook her head.

"You're going to let her get away with it?"

Charlotte stepped back out of the shed and stared at the forest, and at the distant tow-path. Everything seemed so complicated, but there was one option that made the whole mess just go away. She felt that she should stay and help to put things right, but at the same time she craved the freedom and sanity of a quick, easy end to the drama.

"Charlotte?" Ruth continued after a moment. "What are you going to do?"

"I'm going to go home," Charlotte replied, turning back to face her for the last time. "Back to London."

Ruth nodded.

"And I'm going to stay there," Charlotte continued. "I'm going to stay in London and I'm never going to come back here."

"Don't over-react."

"Oh, I think I'm under-reacting right now," Charlotte replied, with tears in her eyes as she forced herself to stay calm. "If I was over-reacting, you'd be missing some teeth by now."

"Tell me your news," Ruth replied, a hint of desperation creeping into her voice as she patted the makeshift bed that she'd provided for Sophie's captivity. "You said earlier that you had something exciting to tell me. Come on. Sit down and give me the gossip. What's happening? Have you met someone?"

Charlotte shook her head. She didn't want her 'news' to have anything to do with Ruth.

"I understand that you're upset," Ruth continued, her voice filled with nervous tension, "but you have to see it from my point of view. I *knew* you weren't Charlotte. I just knew it, in my heart, and I had to prove it. And with Mummy's deteriorating condition, I didn't have long. I knew that once her dementia really took hold, the truth would be lost forever. I had to take drastic action."

"So you imprisoned your daughter for a year," Charlotte replied, shocked by the idea.

"She was happy," Ruth replied, making an extra effort to smile despite the tears in her eyes. "Maybe she was a little bored from time to time, but it was worth it. We had to know the truth, didn't we? I didn't do it for myself, Charlotte. I did it for all of us. Now we can move forward as a family. All that matters is the truth." She paused, waiting for Charlotte to capitulate. "Why don't we talk about Ettolrahc? You used to love Ettolrahc."

"That was the real Charlotte," Charlotte replied. "To me, all that stuff was just bullshit that Mum used to trick me into thinking I was her." She paused. "Not Mum. Helen. I guess it'll take me a while to change that habit. Still, I learned it, so I guess I can unlearn it."

"But you can't abandon your family," Ruth said, her voice full of sweetness-and-light even though there were tears in her eyes. "Family is everything, Charlotte."

"You can't have two, though," Charlotte replied, "can you? And I've got another one waiting for me."

"You're going to look for your biological parents?"

"No."

"Then what?"

"Goodbye, Ruth," Charlotte said calmly.

"But you have to -"

"No," Charlotte said firmly. "I don't. I don't have to come back at all. I never really did anyway. I'm not Charlotte, so I could never come 'back' here. And now I don't have to bother trying to come back ever again." Stepping out of the shed, she turned back and spotted the padlock hanging from the bolt. Before she could really think her actions through, she pushed the door shut and closed the padlock, knowing full well that Ruth had the key inside.

"What are you doing?" Ruth asked, hurrying to the door and trying to push it open. "Charlotte, this is ridiculous. You're being childish!"

Checking that the padlock was secured, Charlotte felt a shiver pass through her body.

"Come on," Ruth continued, "we're not children anymore. Open the door!"

Taking a step back, Charlotte watched as the firmly-bolted door rattled some more. Ruth was trying to get it open, but she had no chance.

"I'll tell Tony to come and let you out," she said after a moment. "Don't worry. You won't be stuck in there for a year. I wouldn't be that fucking cruel."

"Charlotte!" Ruth shouted, still trying to force the door. "Don't be *ridiculous*! Let me out of here!"

"Goodbye," Charlotte whispered. With that, she turned and started walking back toward the house, so she could get to her car and drive away. There was still a part of her that wanted to storm back into that shed and rip her so-called sister apart, but she felt that for once she could control her anger. The path ahead seemed calm and clear, and she knew exactly where she was supposed to be.

"Charlotte!" Ruth shouted from the shed. "Charlotte, come back! Get back here right now!"

"Grow up," Charlotte muttered.

She ignored the calls and shrieks. After all, she figured, these people weren't her family, not really. She had to get away from that house, and back to London. Back to the only people who really mattered anymore. As she reached the fence at the bottom of the garden, she paused to look at the gate. Twice in her life, she'd seen the silhouette of a little girl standing by the gatepost, as if unable to get all the way to the house. Swinging the gate out of her way, Charlotte grabbed a rock and used it to prop the way open.

Feeling another shiver pass through her body, she glanced over her shoulder, half expecting to find someone standing nearby. There was no-one there, of course, but the sensation had felt very real.

"There you go," she whispered, hoping that something nearby might hear her. "There's nothing stopping you. You can go back now, if that's what you really want, but..." She paused. "If you want my advice, you'll stay by the river. Just because you *can* finally go back, doesn't mean you should." She paused again. "I guess it's up to you," she added, before turning and making her way across the lawn. In the distance, her sister was still calling for her to come back. She sounded completely insane, which was, perhaps, the whole point. Ruth had always been highly strung, and she'd finally allowed her anger and bitterness to spill over.

Spotting Tony and Sophie embracing up ahead, Charlotte glanced over her shoulder and saw that the rock had somehow come loose, allowing the wooden gate to swing shut.

Twenty years ago

"What are you doing?"

Startled, Charlotte looked away from the window and saw that her sister Ruth was standing in the doorway, watching. It was late, and they were both supposed to have gone to bed, but Charlotte had instead been standing by the window, staring out at the dark lawn.

"Nothing," she said quietly.

"Are you looking at something?" Ruth asked, making her way across the room until she was standing right next to Charlotte. They both looked out the window for a moment. "What were you looking at?"

"Nothing," Charlotte said again.

"I don't believe you," Ruth replied calmly.

"I thought..." Charlotte paused. "I thought I saw something, that's all. Down at the bottom of the garden."

"Like what?"

"Like... another girl."

Ruth turned and stared at her for a moment. "What kind of girl?"

Charlotte shrugged. She felt as if she couldn't trust Ruth, even though they were supposed to be sisters. There was just something in Ruth's gaze that seemed suspicious and alert, and Charlotte felt that the lack of trust was mutual.

"There can't be another girl in the garden," Ruth said cautiously. "We're the only ones."

"I know," Charlotte replied.

Ruth turned to look back out the window. "So tell me what you saw?"

"It was nothing."

"Tell me."

"I thought I saw..." Charlotte paused again. "I thought I saw a girl, standing down by the gate. I couldn't see her face, but I thought I saw a silhouette. I was watching for a few minutes, and it was like she was trying to come closer, but something was holding her back."

"So she was moving?" Ruth asked.

Charlotte nodded.

"Maybe you *did* see someone," Ruth said after a moment.

"Should we tell Mummy?"

"No."

"Why not?"

Ruth paused. "How big was she?"

"The girl? About the same size as us."

"So it was a little girl?"

Charlotte nodded.

"A little girl standing at the bottom of the garden," Ruth said, seemingly lost in thought, "trying to come back but not able to get past the gate." She paused. "I'm two years older than you, you know," she added eventually. "Two years is a long time, especially when you're young. It's, like, twenty per cent. That makes me smarter, and it means that I understand things better, things that you don't understand at all."

"Like what?"

"Like..." Ruth paused. "Like who that girl was at the bottom of the garden."

"But you said -"

"I know," Ruth said firmly, "but I still know who she was. Well, I think I do."

Charlotte paused. She knew she should ask, but she was scared of the answer. "Who was it?" she asked eventually.

"I'm not telling you," Ruth replied. "Not yet."

"Was it a ghost?"

A flicker of a smile crossed Ruth's lips. "Whose ghost could it be?"

Charlotte opened her mouth to reply, but no words came out.

"Maybe it's my sister's ghost," Ruth said after a moment. "That would make sense, wouldn't it? Maybe she's trying to come back, but something or someone is making it so she can't get through the gate."

"What sister?"

"Charlotte."

"But I'm right here," Charlotte replied tentatively. "I came back."

"Huh," Ruth said, staring intently at her sister. "I suppose so. Then it can't be Charlotte's ghost, can it? Not if you're right here." After a moment, she reached out and touched Charlotte's shoulder, giving it a gentle squeeze as if she was checking that she was solid. "Mummy's weird sometimes," she added. "She says and does weird things. She's been weird since you disappeared, and I think she'll keep being weird. But then, I suppose you're used to that. You know what she's like." She paused. "Don't you?"

Charlotte nodded.

They stood in awkward silence for a moment, two young girls poised at either end of a mystery that neither of them could unravel. Although their shoulders were only a few inches apart as they stood side by side, there seemed to be a gulf between them.

"Maybe it was your ghost friend," Ruth said eventually.

"What ghost friend?" Charlotte asked.

"You don't remember Ettolrahc?"

Charlotte stared at her.

"Some days," Ruth added, "Ettolrahc was all you could talk about. She was your best friend, like a kind of double of yourself. She lived in your body, and it was like..." She paused. "I guess it was like she was your real sister, in a way. Sometimes it was as if you preferred hanging out with her instead of me, even though she wasn't real."

"I don't remember any of that," Charlotte replied blankly.

"Or maybe it was the witch," Ruth added.

Charlotte frowned.

"Don't you remember the witch?"

"Witches aren't real," Charlotte replied. "Neither are ghosts."

Ruth stared at her for a moment. "You really believe that, don't you?"

"Stuff like that is just dumb," Charlotte said.

"I'm sure it'll all come back to you," Ruth continued after a moment, with a faint smile. "I mean, why wouldn't it? But if it doesn't, I guess I can fill you in." She paused. "We should go to bed. Mummy'll get angry if she finds us awake." Heading back over to the door, she glanced back at Charlotte. "Good night. I'm glad you came back. I missed you."

"I missed you too," Charlotte replied, mostly to be polite. She liked Ruth so far, but she felt no affinity with her, no kinship or connection.

Once Ruth had gone back to her own bedroom, Charlotte stayed at the window for a while. She was convinced that the silhouette of the other girl would reappear amongst the shadows at the bottom of the garden, but after a few minutes she realized that perhaps she'd been mistaken all along. There couldn't be a ghost down there, because ghosts only came when someone had died. Taking a deep breath, Charlotte turned and walked over to her bed. Settling under the duvet, she stared at the dark wall and waited to feel tired. She figured it was natural to be a little out of place, after spending a year away. Then again, she felt as if she was in a completely unfamiliar place, and that despite the warm welcome she'd been given, she was completely alone.

Epilogue

"Charlotte?" John shouted. "Is that you?"

Standing in the doorway, Charlotte wasn't quite sure what to say. She quietly placed her backpack on the chair before pushing the door shut, taking off her coat, and then pausing to look at herself in the mirror. The drive back to London had been a blur, and she felt as if she was in a daze.

"Charlotte?"

She opened her mouth to reply, but she didn't know where to even begin explaining things. Still, that name Charlotte kind of seemed appropriate, and she figured she might as well hang onto it. Although she hadn't gone to the police and told them about the whole mess, she *had* done some research into missing children from the Farnborough area twenty years ago, and with a reasonable degree of confidence she'd narrowed her identity down to one of three girls, named Edith, Kylie and Donna. Frankly, she didn't fancy any of those names, and she didn't see the point in making an effort to contact her 'real' family. The past had proven to be a mess so many times, she figured she should just focus on the future.

"I thought I heard you," John said, coming through from the kitchen and kissing her on the cheek. "You're just in time for the best home-made spaghetti bolognese you've ever tasted in your life."

Charlotte smiled weakly, still not knowing what to say.

"You alright?" John asked, placing a hand on her belly. "Did you tell your sister?"

She shook her head.

"Why not?"

"It's none of her business," Charlotte replied. "She's not..." She took a deep breath. "Damn it, I could use a glass of wine right now."

"One wouldn't hurt," John said with a smile. "I'll get -"

"No," Charlotte said, grabbing his arm before he could hurry back to pour her a glass. "I want to do this properly," she continued. "I never even thought I *could* get pregnant, and now that I am, I damn well wanna do it right. No more smoking, no more drinking. I'll go on a fucking detox diet and all that crap, and..." She paused. "Maybe we should try to cut out the swearing too. You know, I've been thinking, and I think you should be aware that I *might* turn out to be an over-protective mother after all. Not, like, overbearingly so, but still... just a tad."

"Doesn't sound too bad," John replied. "If it means anything to you, I'm convinced you're going to be a brilliant mother."

"Not brilliant," she said with quiet satisfaction. "But good, at least. I've had some bad examples to study at close quarters, and I've seen what happens when things go wrong."

"Huh," John said with a smile. "Why so cryptic?"

Instead of replying, she put her arms around him and held him tight. Not *too* tight; after all, she knew she had to be careful not to put too much pressure on her belly. She still had six months to go until her due date, and she was determined to be the best possible mother. It felt like the only good thing that could possibly come out of this whole mess.

"I love you," she whispered.

"I love you too."

"And I promise," she said after a moment, still hugging John, "that I will *never* lock our child in a shed for a year."

"That's, uh, good to hear," John said, sounding a little confused. "So, dinner's pretty much ready. You hungry?"

"Sure," she said, stepping back from the hug. "I'll be through in a moment, okay?"

Once John had gone back into the kitchen, Charlotte made her way over to the mirror that hung at the other end of the hallway. She stared at herself in the harsh electric light and realized, with relief, that she still knew the person who was staring back at her. Sure, her name wasn't *really* Charlotte Abernathy, but that didn't change who she was. It was tempting to go digging through the past and try to find her real family, but she figured the best option was probably to just focus on the future, at least for now. Placing a hand on her belly, she realized that, for the first time, she could actually feel the faintest bump.

She was sick of worrying about people who might or might not come back from places to which they might or might not have gone. It was time, she figured, to focus on new arrivals.

ALSO AVAILABLE

Dark Season: The Complete First Series

When Sophie Hart is rescued from a mugging by a mysterious, silent vampire, she discovers that she is part of a dark prophecy. Patrick is the last vampire on Earth, having killed the rest of his species at the end of a bloody war, and he has plans for Sophie. But will she survive?

This volume collects together the first 8 Dark Season books, covering the entire first series. Along the way, Sophie encounters not only a vampire but also werewolves, ghosts, evil maids with sharp teeth, crazed psychiatrists and dream-sucking Tenderlings. She travels to Gothos, the ancestral home of the vampires. She discovers a secret hidden inside the body of an old woman, and later she finds another dark secret hidden inside her own body.

ALSO AVAILABLE

The Night Girl

When she starts her new job as a night shift assistant, Juliet Collier has no idea that she's about to meet a mysterious entity that lurks in an abandoned part of the building.

Soon, Juliet finds herself granted a gift that means she can kill indiscriminately, and apparently without consequences. Meanwhile, eleven years earlier, a young Juliet makes a terrible mistake that sets her on a dark course.

This is the story of a girl whose decisions lead her to a devastating end-point, as she struggles to reconcile the voices in her head with the reality in front of her eyes.

ALSO AVAILABLE

Devil's Briar

In the remote wilderness of Colorado, Bill and Paula Mitchell discover an entire lost town. Devil's Briar was abandoned many years ago, and has fallen into disrepair. But it soon becomes clear that the town contains some special and highly unusual qualities, and that elements of the past are seeping through into the present.

As she tries to get to the bottom of the mystery, Paula finds herself drawn deeper and deeper into the bizarre time loop that keeps the entire town trapped in eternity. Soon it becomes clear that nothing in Devil's Briar will ever be the same again, and that two time periods are merging with horrific consequences.

ALSO AVAILABLE

Broken Blue

Returning home for her father's funeral, Elly Bradshaw soon finds herself drawn into the dangerous world of billionaire Mark Douglas.

Although she finds Mark irresistible, Elly learns he hides a dark secret. She's quickly pulled deep into a dark sexual game that threatens to change the way she views the world forever. Meanwhile, back in the late nineteenth century, another set of players are caught up in the same game.

Tortured by his role as Mr. Blue, Edward Lockhart sets out to end the game forever. His failure, however, results in the arrival of Jonathan Pope onto the scene. Cynical and only interested in a payday, Pope begins to investigate the shadowy trio of players who keep the game alive.

ABOUT THE AUTHOR

Amy Cross writes horror, paranormal and fantasy novels, although she sometimes stumbles into other genres.

She has been writing all her life, but only started publishing her work in 2011. Since then, she has sold more than 200,000 copies of books such as Asylum, Dark Season and The Girl Who Never Came Back. She lives in the UK.

Printed in Great Britain
by Amazon